by
Eloise Greenfield
Illustrated by
John Steptoe

HarperCollins*Publishers*

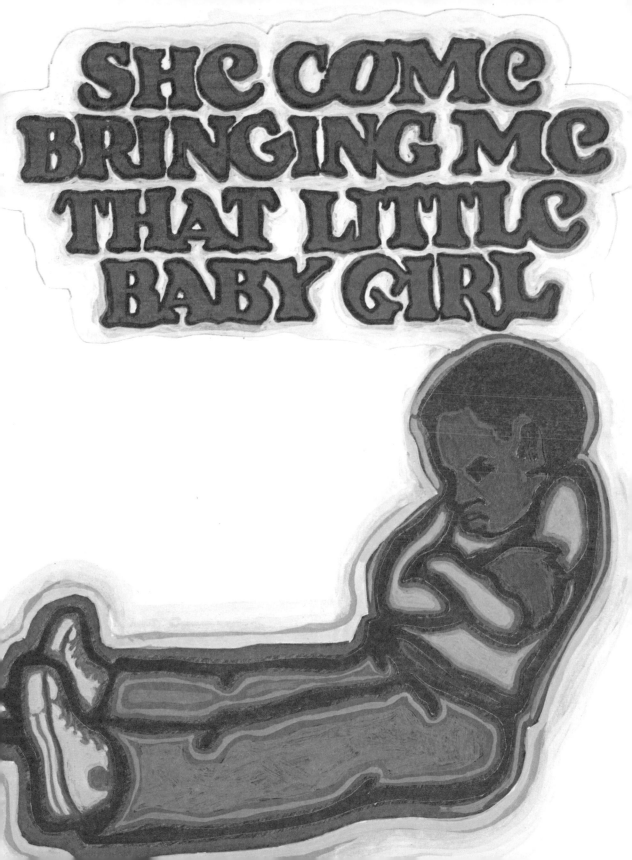

She Come Bringing Me That Little Baby Girl
Text copyright © 1974 by Eloise Greenfield
Illustrations copyright © 1974 by John Steptoe
Printed in the U.S.A. All rights reserved.

Library of Congress Cataloging-in-Publication Data
Greenfield, Eloise.
    She come bringing me that little baby girl.
    Summary: A child's disappointment and jealousy over a new baby
sister are dispelled as he becomes aware of the importance of his new
role as a big brother.
    ISBN 0-397-31586-4.—ISBN 0-397-32478-2 (lib. bdg.)
    ISBN 0-06-443296-3 (pbk.)
    [1. Brothers and sisters—Fiction.]   I. Steptoe, John, date, ill.
II. Title.
PZ7.G845Sh   [E]   74-8104

For Steve and Monica
and all other Black brothers and sisters
who love and take care of each other

I asked Mama to bring me a little brother from the hospital, but she come bringing me that little baby girl wrapped all up in a pink blanket. Me and Aunt Mildred were looking out the window when Daddy brought them home.

I was glad to see Mama even if she didn't bring me what I wanted. When she got out of the car, I ran to the door to meet her.

I didn't like her anyway. She cried too loud.

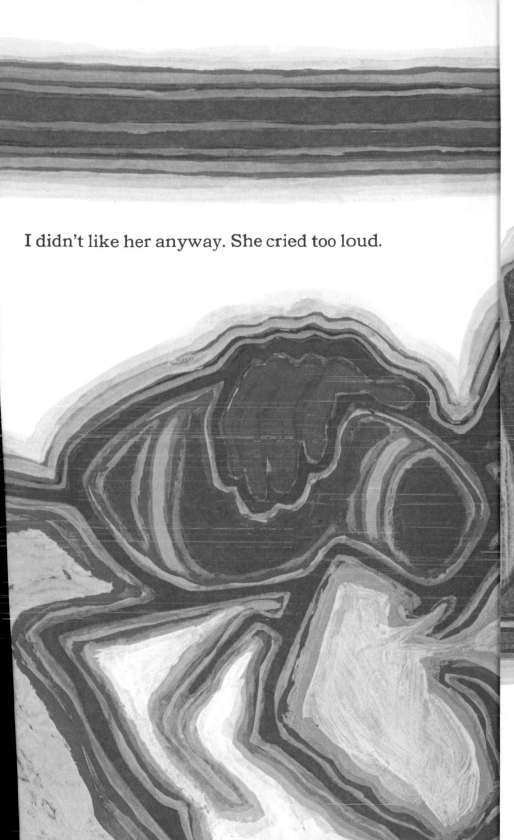

Mama hugged me hard. She was glad to see me, too. But she only had one arm to hug me with 'cause she didn't put that little girl down for a minute.

Daddy helped them upstairs to the bedroom, but he didn't forget me. He said, "Come on, Kevin. We got to see what this baby's all about."

Mama sat on the bed and Aunt Mildred unwrapped the baby real slow and careful. It was a girl, all right, 'cause her fingers were way too small. She'd never be able to throw my football to me.

Not only that, she didn't look new with all those wrinkles in her face.

And not only that, I didn't like the way Mama and Daddy looked at her. Like she was the only baby in the world.

Then Aunt Barbara came with a big box tied in a long shiny ribbon. For the baby. She said, "Hi, Kevin." But she was looking at that little girl when she said it.

And Uncle Roy came with another box. He slapped me on my head and said, "How you doing, man?" But he didn't pick me up and swing me around like he always does.

Mrs. Moore from across the street came, and she had a present, too. She didn't even see me. All she said was, "Where's the baby? Where's the baby?"

It was making me sick to see them crowding around that ugly old baby and making those stupid noises. And presents all over the place. It was really making me sick.

So I put my chair by the window and just sat there, looking out at a squirrel running across the wire. I wasn't thinking about that old squirrel, though. I sure wasn't.

The next thing I know, Mama come bringing me that little baby girl and putting her right in my lap. I didn't even look down at that baby.

Daddy brought Mama a chair and she sat down beside me. She helped me hold the baby with one of her arms and she put her other arm around me.

"You're a big brother now," Mama said.

"I don't want to be a brother to no girl," I said.

"But I need you to help me take care of her," Mama said.

I said, "You do?"

Mama smiled at me and hugged me tight with that one arm. "Yes, I do," she said. "And you know what?"

I said, "What?"

"I used to be a baby girl," she said.

I said, "You did?" I looked up at Mama and down at that baby.

"Uh-huh," Mama said. "And my big brother used to help take care of me."

"I sure did," Uncle Roy said. "I wouldn't let nobody bother my little sister."

I tried to think of how they looked. Mama as a baby and Uncle Roy as a boy. It was so funny, I laughed right out loud.

I couldn't laugh too hard, though. I didn't want to break the baby.

I looked at her again and she wasn't all that ugly anymore. She was a little bit cute, even with the wrinkles.

I gave the baby back to Mama. "I got to go get Kenny and show him my sister," I said.

"Hurry back, man," Uncle Roy said. "You still got that swing coming."

I got Kenny, and Debra too. And they just stood there looking at my sister like they had never seen a baby that pretty before.

I was watching them, though. I had to be sure they didn't squeeze her too hard or anything.

You know, when my sister's fingers grow some, maybe I can show her how to throw a football. If she uses both hands.

And she can have one of Mama's arms, too. As long as she knows the other one is mine.

Canoe Tripping with Kids

David and Judy Harrison

Drawings by NANCY HARRISON

The Stephen Greene Press • Brattleboro, Vermont

With thanks to Christopher Merrill for his help and encouragement and to Shirley Olson for her work on the manuscript. Our greatest debt is to Charles H. and Huntington W., our own mentors.

Produced in the UNITED STATES OF AMERICA.
Designed by DOUGLAS KUBACH.
Published by THE STEPHEN GREENE PRESS,
Fessenden Road, Brattleboro, Vermont 05301.

Library of Congress Cataloging in Publication Data

HARRISON, DAVID, 1938–
  Canoe tripping with kids.

  Includes bibliographical references and index.
  1. Canoes and canoeing.   2. Family recreation.
I. HARRISON, JUDY, 1939–   joint author.   II. Title.
GV789.H37   797.1'22   80-28213
ISBN 0-8289-0426-X (pbk.)

FRONTISPIECE: Black Lake, Saskatchewan, at sunset.

"Ye who love the
Love the sunshin
Love the wind an
And the rain-sho
And the rushing
Through their pa
And the thunder
Whose innumera
Flap like eagles

To you who dre
children, we dea

Contents

Introduction   3

1: Take them along   7

2: Launching your canoe trip   14

3: The canoe trip doesn't start on the water   29

4: Equipment for family canoeing   35

5: Clothing   58

6: Food   66

7: Wildlife   83

8: First aid, safety, and conditioning   89

9: Canoe skills for family tripping   100

10: Underway   125

11: Diversions for the kids   146

12: Living with the inevitable   157

13: For the record   173

14: Yukon Encounter   180

Epilog: Twilight   185

Information sources   189

Index   201

Canoe Tripping with Kids

Introduction

Should you ask me, whence these stories?
Whence these legends and traditions,
With the odors of the forest,
With the dew and damp of meadows,
With the curling smoke of wigwams,
With the rushing of great rivers,
With their frequent repetitions,
And their wild reverberations,
As of thunder in the mountains?
  I should answer, I should tell you.

Why would anyone take his or her family miles from civilization on a canoe trip? What are the rewards of a back-to-nature vacation? Should we take our children? How old should they be? What kind of clothing should one take for children on a canoe trip? Are bears really dangerous? Would my spouse enjoy a canoeing vacation? These questions, and many more, are asked of us each year. There are as many vacation preferences as there are people, but if, like so many of us, you continue to yearn for a retreat which gets the family working and playing together as a team, the family canoe trip may be the answer. If family skiing has bankrupted you, bicycling has exhausted you, and you are still looking for that activity which can accommodate a range of ages and athletic abilities, canoeing has it all.

The canoe is a magic carpet that can carry one beyond the reach of civilization's clatter. By returning to the

* The verse beginning each chapter is from "The Song of Hiawatha" by Henry Wadsworth Longfellow.

3

Black River slough, New Jersey.

slow, self-propelled pace of an earlier time, we make the world grow larger. A week can be spent traversing one hundred miles of river, lake and forest trails—a distance that in today's world is merely a kaleidoscopic blur outside our car window, and only the blink of an eye from a jet at thirty thousand feet.

Canoe tripping expands not only our awareness of an ever-shrinking wilderness, but also our awareness of the family as individuals. A canoe trip may even bring forth long-discarded patterns of interdependence, as members realize that they must do their part in the successful achievement of common goals. The canoe won't go, the dinner won't get cooked, the portage crossed, or the trip completed without teamwork.

Canoe camping is no longer a hardship to be endured only by the hairy-chested outdoorsman. The introduction of new types of food and equipment have made it possible for family canoers to take a measure of comfort into the wilderness with them.

This book provides information for the parent or mentor with some elementary knowledge of the canoe who wishes to take the family, or other youngsters, on a canoeing vaca-

Drifting on the Humptulips River.

tion. We will cover some basics of canoeing technique, but the emphasis is on how to approach the canoe tripping environment—rather than on how to perfect your "J" stroke. The purpose is to provide practical information for parents who seek a rewarding return on their leisure time investment, and who need only a gentle nudge to undertake increasingly adventurous family excursions.

We shall deal with the special needs children have in clothing, food, transportation, and wildlife observation, and the needs parents have in keeping the whole enterprise afloat. There are no fancy recipes or dialogues on the latest in canoeing techniques or equipment. Instead, we offer common sense ideas for making the canoeing vacation a pleasant experience for the whole family.

We have been canoeing as a family for almost two decades. Each chapter deals with the questions we have most often been asked on canoe camping with children. Most of the book is based on our observations of our own children, and of ourselves, through many years of canoeing and camping, on expeditions great and small, in every kind of wilderness environment, in every kind of weather, and with crews ranging in age from toddler to teen, on waters in Canada and the northern United States from Maine to Alaska.

As almost every village, town, and city in our country was founded on or near water, almost every population center is within an easy drive of a river, lake, canal or waterway suitable for canoeing. Rent a canoe, pack up the family and head for a local waterway for a weekend. For a longer vacation, seek out those roadless areas still preserved for our enjoyment. Take along this book, common sense, and a good sense of humor. As you gain the proficiency and teamwork necessary, your family will be able to strike out on those ambitious and challenging adventures which are, after all, life's greatest rewards.

1: Take them along

"Ah, my son!" exclaimed the old man,
"Happy are my eyes to see you.
Sit here on the mat beside me,
Sit here by the dying embers,
Let us pass the night together.
Tell me of your strange adventures,
Of the lands where you have travelled . . . "

" 'Three,' can we go fishing now?" We were only one day, ten miles, a disorganized portage and an as-yet-unmade camp into our two-week canoe trip in the Quetico Provincial Park in southern Ontario. Using a pet name from the time when their grandfather would toss them into the air on the count of three, our son, now aged five, was practicing a time-honored appeal to a willing mentor. "Three" and his grandson both knew that the camp chores could wait. After all, Judy and I would get things organized in our own fashion, while he and David explored new waters with anxious fishing rods. Our daughters, Nancy and Juli, quickly signed on, leaving Judy and me to attend to pitching tents and preparing for dinner.

Only a grandfather's endless patience could cope with three kids, a boatful of tangled lines, arguments over an unclaimed canoe seat, or whose turn to cast; and through it all, manage to land a monster northern pike. "Three" flipped his prize into the canoe where the slimy and spluttering fish churned lines and lures into an insoluble snarl, all to cries of excitement from his admiring audience.

FAMILY CANOEING

Our family album shows "Three" hoisting his pike for the camera as three wide-eyed kids, contemplating perhaps their own triumphs to come, admire their grandfather's exploit. Another small stone is added to the aggregate which binds generation to generation. In addition to needing a sense of roots, children need role models; the father as protector and provider, and the mother as homemaker and care-giver. Dwelling in all of us is a teacher or mentor, the necessary transmitter of wisdom and experience through the generations. In the current cultural preoccupation with "doing your own thing," "finding oneself," and "life style" pursuits, we recognize that such traditional concepts are out of vogue. So be it. We will eventually return to our senses, as a matter of survival.

We think canoeing can satisfy the togetherness impulse and can be initiated while the kids are quite young. It allows for a wide range of skill and endurance among family members and can be done at considerably less expense than other sports. Few other pursuits can offer such a diversity of habitat or certainty of discovery. By canoe, one may explore the pathways of history. Present and future swimmers, hikers, fishermen, birdwatchers, photographers, entomologists and geologists are able to pursue their avocations in remote corners reserved for the canoer's enterprise.

One needs only two inches of water to float a canoe, and it's free. A canoeing friend of mine says that since God created earth one-quarter land and three-quarters water, it seems logical that He intended us to spend three times as much time paddling as we spend walking!

The out-of-car-doorsmen in their wagons and Winnebagos are compelled to carry suburbia into the woods with them. Canoers are far less encumbered. We must admit, however, to taking with us, from time to time, our own links to home—security blankets, both figurative and actual. On a trip to Ontario, our twelve-day voyage over-

8   *Canoe tripping with kids*

lapped our daughter's eighth birthday. Judy recognized the possible trauma of a little girl's missing out on one of life's important events, and accordingly packed along all of the neecssary ingredients for a two-layer birthday cake. Despite a downpour which drenched our campsite, the cake was produced and ceremoniously presented to Juli, who up to that point had every reason to believe that canoe trips forgot about birthdays.

That was the same year that our son, barely four, lost his "blankie." It had been hung out to dry on a bush near our tent. In the early morning we packed up and paddled on, leaving behind this fragrant festoon. Many miles down river the loss was discovered, but there was no going back.

A canoe trip isn't all hard work. Plan the trip to provide some leisure moments. The kids will enjoy it more, too.

David wept and sulked. Never was a river so remote. Time, rather than consoling words, as it turned out, was the best cure.

TAKING KIDS ALONG

When you take the kids along, it's important to carry some support systems and security blankets, particularly in the early years, but a great deal of tempting excess baggage is really unnecessary. It is remarkable how an excursion into the outdoors can ignite young but under-exercised imaginations. Idle hours have been known to produce bows and arrows, daggers and guns, fashioned from forest flotsam; fishing poles, "bear tracks," and bark canoes. With sticks, kids will etch modern history in the earth. Toads, frogs and grasshoppers will be captured, and, when the hunter's ego is satisfied, released.

The capacity for carrying the materials of a comfortable mode of living is one of the attractions of canoe tripping.

Almost any age is the right age—but plan your outing accordingly.

For a day trip, two youngsters will fit amidships, but keep their weight low.

Although one must watch weight to provide freeboard and portageability, canoers are never forced to live like moles or to eat dusty, dehydrated fare. Tents with head room, comfortable bedding, changes of clothing, whole foods—mostly off the supermarket shelves—permit the canoeing party to travel in relative luxury, and make it possible to take the kids along without a drastic reduction in creature comforts.

We urge you to take the kids along and start them young. You and your husband, wife, or fellow mentor should have mastered the basics of canoeing and camping beforehand; and when you start, you should start small. There is no reason why kids can't be included after the diaper phase is passed, but plans and ambitions must be scaled down accordingly. An afternoon spent paddling on a canal, long since deserted of commerce, with a picnic shared on the ancient tow path alongside, is adventure aplenty for a beginning canoe trip.

If you can get them to do the work while you play, you're that much further ahead.

Often one can paddle two or three miles on an otherwise busy lake, round a bend, and find a secluded cove and campsite. The car is barely an hour away, motor boats can be dimly heard, and sails dot the lake, but you and your kids are on a small adventure in your own wilderness niche. Only a half-mile from the campsite, a small creek empties into a marshy estuary, where you can visit in the evening, well after the sailors and water skiers have retired from a cooling, sunset lake. In the quietness of your canoe you may surprise a browsing deer or a beaver on its nightly rounds. Chipmunks arrive to dispose of your child's discarded half of a peanut butter sandwich. To a four-year-old—that's wildlife. A trail leads from the campsite along the lake shore and rises gently to a seldom-visited pond. Even in today's crowded world, a canoe can find these retreats close to the buzz of civilization.

Parents tend to underestimate the ability of kids to adjust, indeed, to thrive in the outdoors environment; a small passenger sleeps on the floor of the canoe, as you make your mileage for the day. A five-year-old can walk a mile portage without thinking much of it—watch them in the back yard sometime. At an early age your kids can be competent, contributing paddlers and partners; the family's togetherness is bound by the dimensions of the canoe.

Over the years, Judy and I have exchanged knowing glances as friends or acquaintances protested that, as soon as their kids were a little older, they, too, would like to take them on a backpacking or canoe trip. We wish them well, but when we discover that the kids are already twelve years old, we know the odds are growing slim. The kids grow up too fast, and just when anxious parents are seized by a belated mentor impulse, they discover ruefully that peer approval activities, puppy love, Little League, soda fountain fraternization, and other pressures of adolescence have put them out of reach. Then, in a twinkling, they are gone.

2: Launching your canoe trip

Thus the Birch Canoe was builded
In the valley by the river,
In the bosom of the forest;
And the forest's life was in it,
All its mystery and its magic,
All the lightness of the birch-tree,
All the toughness of the cedar,
All the larch's supple sinews;
And it floated on the river
Like a yellow leaf in Autumn,
Like a yellow water-lily.

Canoeing is a wonderful way to experience a very special brand of family closeness. It is a means to test the pluck, skill and ingenuity of the whole family, even the very youngest. There will be moments of triumph and discomfort, blissful contentment and exhaustion. Such moments will combine with the events which are the raw material of memories. I must admit, however, that most adventures are more rewarding in the retelling and recollection than in the actual experiencing. I am also reminded that the great arctic explorer, Steffanson, declared that an "adventure" was the result of poor planning.

Our family now looks back with great pride on a grueling day in a park in northern Quebec. We had had great difficulty in gathering sufficient information for our trip, and learned seven days into the trip that we were going in the wrong direction. We found ourselves wading and dragging our canoes up the river as the sun started to sink behind the silhouetted pines. Each new exertion tested our physical limits. Campsites were nonexistent; what should we do? A vote was taken and it was unanimously decided to push three more miles upriver to a lake. Our three children outdid themselves as they hopped into the cold river and helped to drag the canoes upstream and to portage where we could. We finally made camp, very late, very tired, but exhilarated by our accomplishment. We had all taken a step beyond what we thought our capabilities to be.

Of course our adventure was due to bad planning, incomplete maps, and lack of proper information. Fortunately, these deficiencies were offset by a group in good physical condition and with enough experience to know what was called for in the circumstances.

PRELIMINARY PLANS

Assuming your family owns or has access to a canoe and has mastered the basics of canoeing, and that all can swim or are Red Cross "water safe," it's time to make your plans. First, you need to know how much time you wish to take, based on an honest assessment of the family's appetite.

A trip of less than one week should be considered a necessary trial run, perhaps a long weekend. Remember, though, that the same amount of gear, other than food quantities, must be assembled for a three-day trip as for a month-long journey. The trial journey is not a bad idea, in any event, since that's the time to discover that Mom is allergic to down, the fishing reels are out of line, the tent leaks, or that the family can't function without Cocoa Puffs for breakfast.

Your scheduling needs to allow time to get to and from your destined area, and needs to provide for enough days to cover the geography contemplated with some insurance thrown in. While many factors will determine the length of your canoe trip (that is, the part on the water), one simple rule should apply: the more time or distance required to reach your canoeing area, the more time should be spent on the water. Common sense suggests that an 1,800-mile drive to take a one-week canoe trip is a misallocation of energies. In the next chapter we will deal with the problems of Getting There.

Choosing a trip really depends on what you and your family consider to be important, with a high likelihood that there will be a wide variety of wishes and wants to coordinate. At one extreme, depending on skills and physical condition, a challenging semi-ordeal and wilderness experience may be the central theme. At the other, a leisurely week on canals and sheltered waterways could take the family through populated areas. Important factors may be fishing, wildlife spotting, history, or rock hounding. Physical exertion or relaxation, or both, may be goals as well.

Timing

Most canoe trips are planned for the popular vacation months of June, July, and August. This is also the time when all but the most remote waterways are crowded with people operating on similar schedules. In the northern climates the late-August and September through October period has the advantage of fewer people and fewer bugs. Usually after Labor Day they are gone entirely (bugs and people). From ice-out until mid-June one can also beat the flies and people, and fishing at this time is usually tops.

With kids, the later-season trips make more sense, since warmer water and fewer bugs mean more options for family enjoyment. While remoteness may be appealing, some comfort comes from knowing others are at hand. Many years ago, struggling over a steep half-mile portage between two lakes in the Quetico, Dave and I were having to triple the portage. The kids were too small to carry any

Canoes on the Fond du Lac.

more than a small rucksack. We returned exhausted for our third load to find that two Boy Scouts (honest) had materialized on the trail and were heaving up our final packs. They had taken note of our efforts and, with hardly a word, intervened to assist us.

WHERE TO GO

Once the time factor for your trip has been established, you need a location. If this is a first-time trip, consider the national, state or provincial parks, but be sure to write or phone the destination of your choice for additional information. If it is a park, request information on the number of canoe routes, maps, likely number of canoeists using the park, and the names of outfitters in the area. The next step would be to write or phone outfitters and inquire about the variety of trips—flat water, rivers, lakes, number of portages, and the cost for renting all or part of the outfit. Additionally, you may want accommodations for the night before you leave and the day you return. Other sources of information are local Chambers of Commerce, U.S. Department of the Interior, tourist information, and magazines for the canoeist. The magazines often have accounts of trips and information on where to go. For the more advanced trips, trip notes made by previous parties on a selected route are often more accurate and more informative than maps or second-hand reports.

Our own canoe tripping experience has followed a natural progression toward greater distance and difficulty. When Dave and I took our first ten-day canoe trip without the kids we learned a lot about canoeing and ourselves. As a good place to start, we chose Algonquin Park, north of Toronto, using all rental equipment (except for our own sleeping bags and toothbrushes). Outfitted with an aluminum canoe and some friendly advice from the outfitter, we tackled a canoe route suitable to our ambitions but not to our abilities. We did learn, however, and it was because of the early mistakes that we could later plan for trips to include the children. Next came short trips in the Adirondacks, lake chains, or three-day excursions on meandering streams. The key to success is to crawl before walking; biting off more than one can chew is a danger. An unpleasant ordeal may sour the family forever, so use common sense in your planning process.

MAPS AND OTHER INFORMATION SOURCES

You will certainly have better sense than to plunge into an enterprise beyond your skills. Plan well in advance. Good maps and reliable information are extremely important. For the state and provincial parks or wilderness waterways reserved for canoeing there are usually special maps showing the canoe routes, portage trails, campsite locations, and access points (see Appendix 1 for a listing of these Waterways Guides). Outside of such areas, or as a complement to the special maps, both the U.S. Geological Survey and the Canadian Department of Mines and Forests provide free map indexes and order forms for extraordinarily detailed maps. By writing to either of these sources, perhaps specifying the state, province or region of your concern, you will receive free indexes and ordering information. The ideal map scales are 1:250,000 (approximately four miles to the inch) and 1:62,500 (approximately one mile to the inch). Scales larger than this—such as 1:24,000—are fun to follow, but it takes a lot of sheets to cover the area of more than a one- or two-day trip. Smaller scales (1:500,000) lack sufficient detail for the canoeist.

The well-known topographical maps of the U.S. Geological Survey are super for detailing contours, but often inconclusive as to the difficulty of a river. There are plenty of clues for the experienced map reader and river runner, but it is very important to supplement the maps with first-hand information or trip notes of an earlier party. Just a suggestion on the information-gathering process: written inquiry and correspondence, initiated well in advance of your expedition, can generate much of the necessary information; but more often, phone calls directly to the outfitter, fish and game department, float plane operator, or previous expeditioner will fill in the inevitable blanks. As the frequent recipient of requests for trip information, I am inclined to be stingy in my epistles but a veritable magpie on the phone.

In addition to the functional kinds of information gathered for a canoe trip, there is a wealth of reading and research one can undertake for an even more rewarding experience. The history, geology, fauna and flora of your chosen area add to the enjoyment of both the planning and execution of your trip. In some cases, it may be the inspiration. Pierre Berton's thrilling and definitive book, *Klondike Fever*, set the wheels in motion for our family trip to the Yukon (see Chapter 14). Dillon Wallace's turn-of-the-century story of a tragedy in the Labrador wilderness was the tickler for our later excursions into that forbidding country. John McPhee's delightful book on the Pine Barrens make a weekend of canoeing the little rivers of southern New Jersey an enduring pleasure.

Whether you launch your canoe trip near or far, for a weekend or a fortnight, planning your way there should be half the fun. Each discovery is a box which holds still another box. Keep opening them until you have yourself a trip.

PLANNING A TRIP TO THE OZARKS

I've never been to the Ozarks, but it's winter in Chicago, with damp winds swirling in off Lake Michigan adding to the thawing and freezing, and sooty accumulations of urban snow. Anyplace seems like a better place to be than here. The kids are climbing the walls, and Judy lobbies regularly for a trip to the "islands," which of course we can't afford. My own reveries are more modest, as I thumb through some back issues of one of the canoeing magazines. Here's one with a group of grinning kids, huddled under a turned-up canoe, captioned, "Kids 'n Canoes —Or Why Are These Kids Smiling?" Good question. Our two kids are in the process of pulling each other's hair out in the next room—apparently a dispute over the choice of two socially unredeeming TV shows.

The author—a woman—makes some good points, but it's another article that really catches my eye. Chicago in winter is varying shades of gray. A red mill, its water wheel driven by the crystal waters of an Ozark river and framed in the verdancy of oaks and moss, invites me to read about the rivers of Missouri. Missouri has always been St. Louis to me. I had forgotten about the southern section, thinly populated, heavily forested. Normally, I look north when thinking canoe tripping, but it's winter in Chicago and it's going to be winter up North for many months to come. This family had better make some plans now, and look for a trip which gets us out sooner rather than later. I have a week of vacation coming, and if spring is starting to break five hundred miles to the south of Chicago between mid-March and mid-April, there may still be time to plan a trip and get Judy's and the kids' minds off of winter gray and the TV.

They like the idea. We are all willing to grasp at any faint hope that somewhere there is beauty, serenity, sunshine and color, and even if we can't be transported there instantly, we can plan and dream and forget about the cold and grayness all about us. But all we have at this point is an idea. We've never been further south than St. Louis, so we have a lot of research to do.

The article in the canoeing magazine gives a thumbnail sketch of Missouri and its various river systems, but from this we can determine only that we would be interested in rivers in the Ozark region, a pretty fair chunk of geography. It has a magical sound to us; water wheels, grist mills, oak and pine forests, and place names like Alley Spring and Stink Pond. Thick forests; spontaneous, gurgling springs; caves; the land of Huck Finn. We're hooked already.

According to the article we can write to the Missouri Department of Conservation, P.O. Box 180, Jefferson City, Missouri 65102, and for the unbelievably low price of one dollar, receive the 1978 edition of the guide book, *Missouri Ozark Waterways*—114 pages of trip descriptions, maps, and other references. Missouri must be interested in canoers. It takes exactly one week for the book to arrive. The book describes sixty-five trips covering about fortyseven rivers—all in the southern half of the state. We read and reread the book; first, enthralled by the possibilities of this river, then convinced that another is just the one for us.

Since we are planning to be out a week, we want a river that gets us away from the populated areas and into wilder surroundings. We are attracted to the rivers which lie within the state and national forests, and particularly those that now have been included in the Wild and Scenic Rivers system. But we are also aware that other canoers will be similarly attracted to this area. We can find all the traffic and human intercourse we need in Chicago and its suburbs, without seeking an Ozark version of human hubbub. Perhaps the answer will lie in our timing. An early spring start will put us ahead of the summer vacation crowds, and even if we have to pull our two daughters out of school for five days, we can justify that move, knowing that the historic Ozarks will offer them an opportunity to see and learn. With luck, there will be some overlap with their spring break. Anyway, let's get some more facts and worry about that later.

In order to focus our research, we narrow our interests down to the Ozark National Rivers—Taum Sauk Region, in the southeastern part of the state, on the northern border of Arkansas. We will be deep in the Ozarks, but still only a full day's drive (eleven hours, to be exact) from home. Two rivers, the Current and the Eleven Point, seem to combine the requisites of historic interest, canoeable distance, wildness and accessibility to attract us. Also, like most of the Missouri rivers, they are graded Class I and II (easiest and easier), which is appropriate to our family skill level. Judy and I will each take a canoe with a seven- and eight-year-old daughter, respectively, in our bow. No portages. That's a blessing. We can get in plenty of miles and use our backpacking gear and big wooden box for our food. No need to spend a lot of money on freeze-dried fare. Weight's not a problem, so we can pretty much outfit ourselves right at the local grocery store. But we are getting a little ahead of ourselves.

Our guide book lists a number of sources, and I send off letters to the following:

Supervisor
National Forests in Missouri
P.O. Box 937
Rolla, MO 65401

Gentlemen:

Please send me available literature and maps with respect to the Current, Jack's Fork, and Eleven Point rivers. We are planning a canoe trip for Spring of '80.
Thank you for your assistance.

Sincerely,

Division of Tourism
P.O. Box 1055
Jefferson City, MO. 65101

Gentlemen:

I am looking for information about canoe rentals in the vicinity of the Current and Eleven Point rivers. I understand that a list of outfitters is available through your office.

Sincerely,

Denver Distribution Section
Geological Survey
Building 25, Denver Fed. Ctr.
Denver, CO 80225

Gentlemen:

Please send me map indexes for Missouri and Arkansas— topo's of 1:50,000 (1:62,500?) or 1:200,000. I also need order forms.
Thanks for your assistance.

Sincerely,

Just to be safe, I also order maps from the state:

Missouri Department of Natural Resources
Division of Geology & Land Survey
Buehler Park
Rolla, MO 65401

Gentlemen:

Enclosed is $28.00 to cover costs and mailing for the following quadrangles: Montauk, Cedargrove, Lewis Hollow, Round Spring, Eminence.
Thanks for your assistance.

Sincerely,

The last letter is a good example of overeagerness on my part. I thought I might speed up the research process by

My letters of inquiry brought forth a blizzard of information, including an envelope from the Missouri Division of Tourism proclaiming that "Missouri is for Kids Like You"!

sending a check and ordering right off the bat. Back came my check with a very nice note, to the effect that some of these quadrangles were no longer in print, or were not available in certain scales, etc., and furthermore, the $28 was too much money; they can only handle the exact amount (we all know how a bureaucracy works). They kindly enclosed a map index for the state and some order forms, so that I ultimately ended up with duplicate sets; one from the Missouri Department and one from the Denver Section of the U.S. Geological Survey. Armed with the new indexes and order forms, I sent off a $17.50 check for fourteen maps, most of which were 7½-minute maps (1:24,000, or about one-half mile to the inch), and a number of older quadrangles—the surveys are continually being updated—which were 15-minute scale (1:62,500 or about one mile to the inch).

The quadrangles are put aside for the moment, as we begin to sort through the blizzard of other materials that our brief correspondence has generated. The most important is the road map of the state of Missouri, which gives us the orientation of waterways, roads, distances to and from populated areas, and between put-ins and take-outs. Studying the road map, as well as the descriptions of the Current River contained in the *Ozark Riverways* pamphlet, and the descriptive pamphlet on the *Eleven Point—National Scenic River*, confirms our earlier thinking about their overall suitability. (The abundance of publicity also confirms the importance of making our trip in the off-season to avoid the crowds.)

Were we planning a trip to an extremely remote region, where information was scarce or unavailable, the quadrangles would be an absolute must. But for the popular, canoeable waterways of the Ozarks, there is plenty of printed and first-hand information to answer most of the questions about access, egress, topography, river gradient and difficulty. Attention to the topographic maps can wait until we are about to embark downriver, as a complement to other guide books and local information. Underway, however, the topos will permit us to pinpoint the locations of interest, whose whereabouts are imprecisely described in other sources.

By this time our enthusiasm is at a high pitch. The idea born only a short time ago is beginning to look like an achievable reality. We own one fifteen-foot, wood and canvas canoe, but by this time our family of four has outgrown it, so we will need to rent a second canoe. This will be the year to get the kids into the paddling act, rather than carrying them as baggage.

The pamphlet, *Missouri Float Fishing & Canoeing Outfitters,* lists a surprising number of outfitters and rental outlets, so we pick one that appears to be centrally located. In addition to a canoe, we will need a way to get to our put-ins, or be picked up at our take-out (since we are planning to do two rivers, the problem is compounded). More importantly, I want to talk to a human being who can answer some questions about the rivers and the season, the campsites, and traffic.

My phone call to Two Rivers Outfitters gets redirected to the winter residence of the proprietors, and I talk to the wife of the husband/wife team who have operated this particular outfitting service for seven seasons (apparently the business dates back thirty years). She confirms that mid-March to mid-April will get us on the rivers ahead of the main body of tourists, but she also acknowledges that every now and then these parts can get a spring snow storm. (Somehow, a late spring snow on an Ozark canoe trip is more appealing than the Chicago variety, as romance begins to overpower reality.) I jump at my informant's statement, however, that this period can also be one of sunny and delightful weather.

I have expressed interest in having higher water, so that we can begin our trips in the upper, wilder reaches of the rivers. Darleen, who is my informant, confirms the likelihood of this, if we come earlier, rather than later. In response to my question, she also admits that we will need

Canoe tripping with kids

to be on the lookout for downed trees and "rootwads," which can entrap unwary canoeists. The water temperatures should be in the sixties. Although many people do filter or purify the water from the river for drinking, just as many drink right out of the rivers or the springs which constantly feed them. Fishing is not so hot in the main sections of the river, but the upper stretches may produce some trout. The Eleven Point is reputed to have better trout fishing than the Current. I make a mental note. We are planning a swift trip, so fishing is a secondary consideration.

Darleen tells me that there will be no bugs or snakes,* and that we will probably be a little ahead of the actual bloom of spring. Nevertheless, spring could come a little earlier this year; they've had a warmer winter, after several winters of record severity. Overnight accommodations are available in Eminence at the Riverside or the Pine Crest Motels, and there are several grocery stores if we need to pick up last-minute supplies.

Two Rivers Outfitters' canoe rental rates are ten dollars per day, including life jackets (PFD's) and paddles, and they will provide shuttle service at sixteen dollars for the first canoe and four dollars for each additional canoe, for the first trip, and at fifteen dollars for each additional pickup (regardless of the number of canoes) after that. A quick calculation tells me that my rental and shuttle costs are going to be about $135. In fact, total costs will be as follows:

Rental and shuttle	$135
Gas; Chicago to Eminence, Missouri	$100
Motels and meals	$160
Trip food	$100
(over our normal week's food budget)	

* She may have been referring to *our* canoe trip early in the season. Other literature mentions a wide variety of poisonous and nonpoisonous snakes, tarantulas, scorpions, ticks and chiggers as inhabitants of the region.

| Other gear | $150 |
| (someone always needs a new pair of boots, etc.) | |

TOTAL Trip Expense $645

Well, that's not cheap, but it sure beats the "islands," and the kids get to join us. At least we are encouraged enough to set down an itinerary. In the meantime, Darleen will send us a copy of their brochure, giving rates and other information, and she has assured us that for the period of our contemplated trip, only a few days' notice will be necessary to reserve a canoe.

We make up a tentative itinerary. Leave Chicago Friday night at eight P.M. and drive all night (464 miles) to arrive in Eminence at seven or eight on Saturday morning. The kids will sleep the entire way down, and Judy and I can trade off sleeping and driving. We can check into the motel on Saturday morning, and arrange for the canoe rental and the shuttle; pick up the last-minute supplies, and get the general lay of the land; perhaps chat with a few of the local people.

Early Sunday morning we will put into the Jack's Fork at Highway 17 and plan a four days' paddle, two of which will bring us to the confluence with the Current River, arriving at the take-out at Big Spring on Wednesday—a total distance of seventy-eight miles.

If the shuttle can pick us up about two P.M. on Wednesday we can be taken to the put-in for the Eleven Point River at Highway Y. From there it is a thirty-four mile float to the Missouri–Arkansas line, which we should be able to do easily in two days. We can either spend Wednesday night at the put-in or, perhaps, a short distance down river. That will give us Thursday and Friday on the river, and we will make plans to be picked up either late on Friday or early Saturday. We've got a day of insurance in there. At the latest, we would be spending Saturday night at the motel in Eminence, leaving early on Sunday morning for the all-day drive home to Chicago.

We will probably arrive home just in time for the last snowstorm of the season. Oh well.

3: The canoe trip doesn't start on the water!

Gitche Manito, the mighty,
The creator of the nations,
Looked upon them with compassion,
With paternal love and pity;
Looked upon their wrath and wrangling
But as quarrels among children,
But as feuds and fights of children!
Over them he stretched his right hand,
To subdue their stubborn natures,
To allay their thirst and fever.

How many canoe trips are doomed from the start by long hours on the road, battling traffic, while Mom and Dad referee battles without armistice raging in the back seat? Often these internecine struggles are exhausting to the point of overshadowing the rewards of the canoe trip. How often have you heard, "It's my turn by the window." "Nancy is sitting on my share of the seat." "When will we be there?" "How come Nancy and Juli always get the windows?" "I'm thirsty!" "I have to go to the bathroom!"—always announced eight minutes after leaving the last gas stop.

GETTING THERE: TRAVELING WITH KIDS

There are no fool-proof recipes for happy traveling with children, and the alternative approaches to this problem are necessarily limited. One can point the car in the direction of the put-in, grit the teeth, hope for the best and take off; or one can plan the trip from home to put-in as carefully as one plans the actual voyage. The canoe trip planner tends to think in terms of beginning at the put-in and ending at the take-out, but with children along, one has to think ahead. Whether the car ride is for two hours to the local canal, or a week to the Yukon Territories; whether travel is by car, train, plane, or boat; the kids get bored, tired, contentious, and hungry, making the trip an endurance contest for all. Here are a few helpful suggestions on traveling with children:

When packing the car, consider the kids; their ages and the length of time they will be confined in the car will dictate the layout. To help make the trip more pleasant for all, they need room to spread out, room to sleep in, room to play and room to eat. Think big! Allow as much space as possible. Even a VW Bug can be turned into a playroom by removing the back seat and replacing it with a mattress or a rug. Then pack the gear in such a manner that the little ones have enough room to stretch out. It may even be possible to provide a smooth writing or drawing surface by the careful placement of the gear.

Food seems to be the most reliable method of distracting fidgety kids. Forget the three-meals-a-day routine. The torpor induced by keeping the kids well stuffed may even put them to sleep! Fruit, sandwiches, carrots and celery sticks, raisins, little boxes of cereal are all good finger foods that aren't too sticky or messy. Packages of premoistened tissues come in handy to clean off grubby little hands and faces, and can be easily disposed of in the car litter bag.

Next to incessant, gnawing hunger, the lack of physical activity seems to be the most common cause of juvenile fidgets. The gas stop is one opportunity to let the kids out to let off some of that steam. Take a few minutes and really run the gang around. Frisbie for the older children and jump rope and races for the smaller ones will give them a brief, strenuous workout.

Recalling gas stops I have known, there are some dangers, which may be compounded by more kids or the use of two or more cars if you happen to be a multi-family trek. On one memorable occasion, we had stopped at the last gas station before civilization petered out entirely, in the heart of French-speaking Quebec. The kids did their laps as we gassed up, bought one last soda pop and a few fishing lures, and took advantage of the last flush toilets before disappearing into the bush for a week.

We were spread out in two cars; four adults and three children. It was five miles of billowing dust and spraying gravel after we got under way again that I counted the heads in the car ahead of us, and timorously inquired as to our eight-year-old daughter's whereabouts. "Must be in Alex's car," my husband responded. Not entirely convinced of that, I urged him to honk Alex over. Sure enough, no Nancy. Flying back down the road, we were intercepted by one of the locals, chasing after us with a very scared little Nancy in tow. That taught me once-and-for-all to do the head-count before and not after the caravan gets under way.

You may find that the kids are wound up and have a hard time settling down once back in the car after a stop, so why not take advantage of their high spirits and sing. Everyone has a favorite song; even the very smallest member of the group. Take turns and sing everyone's favorite. The kids seem to love the round-type songs. "One Hundred Kids in a Bed and Middle One Said Roll Over and They All Rolled Over and One Fell Out," is usually accompanied by great shouts of glee.

There are also lots of car games for all ages to play. One game that has worked well for us is adding the last digit of license plate numbers until someone reaches one hundred. Along the same line, try completing the letters of the alphabet from off the license plates until Z is reached. Another old favorite is finding the plates from all fifty states, a project that may well span the whole trip, coming and going. There are also many commercial car games available, such as Auto Bingo. Paper games include tic-tac-toe, hang-man and the dot-connecting game.

For the tiny members of the group, try a surprise bag. This is a collection of things to entertain the kids in the car while traveling. This instant entertainment center can be packed in small lunch boxes, shoe boxes, paper bags or whatever. What to put in a surprise bag will be determined by your child's age and special interests. An older child could help pack his own surprise bag. Some suggestions for inclusion are:

Playing cards and educational cards
Scotch tape
Construction paper
Scissors
Christmas or Easter Seals (to stick on blank paper)
Unlined paper
Books (to read aloud, for reading, to look at, follow the dots, etc.)
Pipe cleaners
Crayons (big fat ones—remember, they can melt—take felt pens instead)
Coloring books
Magnet
Magic Slate
Miniature doll family
Stuffed animals
Miniature cars and trucks
Spools and string or yarn

Be sure to bring along that special "blankie" or toy. These

Canoe tripping with kids

things are a child's link with home and security, and are especially comforting when the child is faced with many new situations.

LONG HAULS

If the trip is long distance, consider driving all night so the kids can sleep. We drove from our home in New Jersey to the Quetico–Superior National Forest in northern Minnesota for our canoeing vacation two summers running. Our youngest was four for the first of these trips. We chose to leave New Jersey in the evening, have a picnic dinner on the road, and, trading off sleeping and driving with my husband, we drove all night. When the kids awoke for breakfast, we had already logged fourteen hours of driving. Since they hadn't had a chance to explore their toys and surprises, there was a full day of pleasant driving before we stopped for the night. Everyone helped pick out a motel, with a swimming pool, of course. By stopping early, we all had time for a much-needed frolic in the pool, and, after a good dinner, an overdue night's sleep for Mom and Dad. The overnight stop also gave us an opportunity to sweep out the VW bus, replenish the surprise bag and restock the cooler with a few goodies. It was a short drive the following day, so we arrived at our put-in in Ely refreshed and ready for vacation. For the return trip, we refilled the cooler, and after being in the woods for two weeks, the children were delighted to rediscover the surprise bag.

A few years back an advertising slogan for one of the shipping lines announced that Getting There Is Half the Fun. We had opportunity later to test the thesis by getting the whole family and half a ton of gear from New Jersey to Whitehorse in the Yukon Territories, a distance of almost four thousand miles! Even if we had owned a car that could make it that distance, we had neither the time or mental toughness to cope with a car trip of that duration. Over a year was spent in planning the logistics for that one. The food and gear were shipped by REA two months prior to our own departure. To get the family there, we drove to Montreal, rode the Canadian National Railroad to Edmonton, Alberta, flew by jet to Whitehorse, Yukon Territories, paddled five hundred miles to Dawson City, and returned by DC-3 and jet a month later —a total distance of over nine thousand miles by car, train, propeller and jet plane and, of course, by canoe. Getting there was not only half the fun, it was half the planning.

The same principles for car travel can be applied on the train for keeping the youngsters happy and busy. We packed the surprise bag for David Jr., and the girls brought along their knitting, and packed their own surprise bag with a good supply of books, cards and games. All three children managed to keep themselves entertained for three days; no small feat. Making the job easier, we had a train crew who seemed to go out of their way to make the trip pleasant for everyone. David Jr., age six, was "hired on" by the waiters in the dining car, and also given responsibility for dispensing peanuts and emptying ashtrays in the lounge car.

We arrived in Edmonton after four days on the train, having passed through three time zones, enthusiastic and relaxed. If you have not been on a train in thirty years, or ever, give it a try. We found it to be an extraordinarily relaxing experience, giving time to prepare ourselves mentally for the next lap of our adventure.

On still another trip, we took a spur-of-the-moment detour which lengthened the trip in miles but psychologically shortened it greatly. Forgoing our outbound route along the north shore of the St. Lawrence, we boarded a ferryboat at Baie Comeau, Quebec, for a two-hour crossing of the St. Lawrence. Apparently, the ferry crossing is a bit of an event. A party atmosphere prevailed as a fiddler sawed out a raucous medley below decks. What a welcome diversion after two weeks in the bush, and an unexpected break in the much-dreaded return drive.

When planning any canoe trip, give as much thought

Canoe tripping with kids

and planning to the getting there and getting home as you do to the actual trip, and once underway, don't rule out worthwhile detours such as our ferry crossing. The family canoe trip and the incidental journeys can be a wonderful experience if good planning, common sense and a good sense of humor are exercised.

4: Equipment for family canoeing

Give me of your bark, O Birch-tree!
Of your yellow bark, O Birch-tree!
Growing by the rushing river,
Tall and stately in the valley!
I a light canoe will build me,
Build a swift Cheemaun for sailing,
That shall float upon the river,
Like a yellow leaf in Autumn,
Like a yellow water-lily!

Building your own birchbark canoe could be a fascinating project, but it's hardly a necessary one. Considering its tremendous versatility, the canoe is a bargain. If you have contemplated the investments required by family skiing, biking or backpacking, canoeing will look too good to be true.

Having made that claim, we must admit that, as in most recreational pursuits, there are also opportunities to spend

35

1. CAR RACK COMMERCIALLY AVAILABLE.

2. SLEEPING BAG.

3. CANOE ☆ Light Weight ☆ Recreational

KIDS and EQUIPMENT

4. PACKS

5. PADDLES

6. TENTS

7. LIFE JACKETS ☆ ALSO FLOTATION BELTS WHICH CAN ALSO SERVE AS PILLOWS.

a bundle on canoes and canoe gear. The basic, utilitarian outfit which served our family well for years was gradually replaced by canoes, paddles and other gear that were larger, lighter, stronger, prettier, drier, fancier (who needs an altimeter/barometer?), or in some cases, just newer and more expensive. But some of us are freakier about our equipment than others. Others take pride in "making do" with the old standby, regardless of the size of their bank account. Still others will hang onto a cherished piece of equipment patched many times over, temperamental, or burnished with age; and then rush to buy a fifty-dollar Gore–Tex paddling jacket, complete with a racing stripe.

We're not going to suggest a budget or offer a gospel of equipment requirements, but we will try to pass on our preferences, based on a discovery process many years in the making. As a general observation, we would urge you to shop for quality, and be willing to pay for it. Canoeing, and canoe tripping, should be lifetime activities, and much of your equipment should last a lifetime. Canoeing, especially canoeing with kids, tends to be rough on gear, so one should be somewhat wary of the "go-light" extremes which have been dictated by the constraints of backpacking or bicycling.

RACKS AND ROPES

You can tie your canoe right on top of your sedan or wagon, with padding under the gunwales, and ropes around fore and aft sections run through the car windows; or there are commercially available Ethafoam blocks, grooved to slip onto the canoe gunwale. For the success of both these arrangements you will also need to secure a taut triangle of rope from bow and stern to either end of the front and rear bumpers.

The best canoe racks are those which attach securely to car rain gutters by means of sturdy brackets. I prefer a wooden crossbar (up to a two by four) long enough to carry two canoes side by side. In the case of a rack for either one or two canoes, wooden blocks fixed to prevent lateral movement of the boat are a good idea. These racks also require a taut line at bow and stern as described above. You want to eliminate as much as possible the play between rack and car, and canoe(s) and rack. A good-diameter nylon rope, rather than clothesline, will give you something to yank on, and can be knotted and unknotted without using your fingernails.

Many of us are driving smaller cars than we used to. There are few cars that cannot accommodate at least one full-sized canoe, but with a small car you should be even more certain that your racks and ropes are well secured. Organize things so that the canoe is as level as possible (at least not tilted back) and that the cross bars are as far apart as you can get them. Rubber or neoprene cemented to the top of the crossbar will protect the gunwales, eliminate slipping and provide a quieter carriage. Don't be overly concerned about the canoe overhang at front and rear of your car, as long as both ends of the canoe are tautly roped (the triangle mentioned above) to the bumpers. Vision out the front windshield is seldom impeded, but you might want to hang a red flag off the back of your canoe if it extends three feet or more beyond the rear of the car.

Two-by-fours bolted to heavy-duty brackets which clamp to the rain gutters provide a sturdy rack for two canoes. Note the blocks which prevent lateral movement of the canoe.

CANOES

There are enough canoe designs and materials choices to baffle an engineer or a chemist. Some make sense for family canoeing and some don't. Let's start with the design or shape of the canoe, since you have got a specific purpose in mind. You are looking for a recreational design, which combines stability, ample capacity, undemanding paddleability, and reasonably light weight.

Without being a barge, the canoe must be stable enough so that lurching children or a momentary lapse of attentiveness on someone's part isn't going to put everybody in the drink. On the other hand, as everyone's proficiency grows, the enjoyment of more refined hulls becomes possible. A stable canoe is likely to have a corresponding ample capacity, so no compromise there, but don't rely unquestioningly on the manufacturer's claims, either. There are, fortunately, plenty of canoes meeting a broad range of requirements, including the ability to accommodate two adults and two small children, or one youngster up to twelve or thirteen years of age, plus all the food and gear for a one-week trip.

A canoe with "paddleability" means one that requires no special handling, and whose design is meant for the widest range of uses and waters. It is neither designed for whitewater slalom, nor for marathon racing; the former evidenced by a well-curved, or "rockered" bottom, and the latter by a long, straight-keeled, Vee hull.

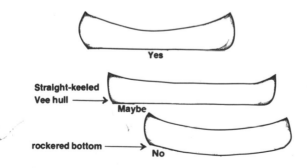

Yes

Straight-keeled
Vee hull ——→
Maybe

rockered bottom ——→ No

The toughest compromise will be the weight of the canoe, which we have now to some extent determined by requiring that the canoe be stable and commodious. In discussing materials, we will see some of the options, but with respect to design, we would opt for a larger canoe at a corresponding increase in weight.

Well, so far, what have we got? Translated into dimensions and weight, we will have a canoe 17 feet long, 36 inches wide at the beam (center thwart), 15 inches deep, and weighing about 75 pounds; its capacity will be 800–900 pounds. A keel is optional, but the keel line will have a very gentle rocker, and the hull will have a modest bulge at the water line—at least in the mid-section—and the upturn at the bow and stern will be noticeable, but not severe.

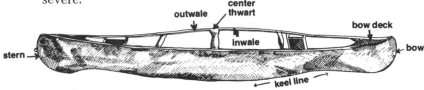

If you are shopping for a canoe and the salesman shows you a boat that is under 16 feet, or over 18 feet, in length; less than 34 inches at the beam, or more than 37 inches; less than 13 inches deep; weighing more than 80 pounds, or exhibiting any extremities of design suggestive of specialized purpose or designer ignorance (there is plenty of the latter around) you had better ask him to explain. If it doesn't make any sense, look for another dealer, preferably one who specializes in canoeing, rather than bowling, hunting, and badminton.

The principal canoe materials today are wood, aluminum, ABS Royalex,* fiberglass, and Kevlar (DuPont trademark). Utility, durability, and reasonableness of price are

---

* A multi-laminated sandwich of vinyl and ABS (acrylonite-butadiene-styrene) with a closed cell foam core. It is also the brand name of Uniroyal and dubbed "Oltonar" by Old Town. Other canoe manufacturers use the Royalex or their own name.

hallmarks of aluminum and ABS, with the latter rapidly making headway on aluminum as the popular choice for recreational canoeing. Weight is liable to be the compromise with these materials, however—they are relatively heavy. Fiberglass offers the greatest number of hull design options, and is often the choice when a custom application is desired. You need to know the builder, and exactly what you are looking for in fiberglass, however, since the market also boasts an array of cheap and imprudent designs.

The Mercedes and BMWs of canoedom are hulls in wood and Kevlar. Wood is appealing for its warmth and aesthetic qualities—as well as a surprising abundance of designs—and Kevlar represents the ultimate in light weight and high strength. Kevlar is a DuPont aramid fiber woven into a cloth but having greater tensile strength and resistance to tearing and abrasion than fiberglass. For either a wood or a Kevlar boat, you can expect to pay a thousand dollars, or more. There is nothing quite so satisfying to the eye as a fine wood canoe, but for family use or canoe tripping, there may be better choices. If you are willing to spend the money, there are some very fine Kevlar canoes falling within the design parameters mentioned earlier, and the only thing likely to be compromised is your pocketbook.

While there are some excellent all-round designs in aluminum—and it is maintenance-free—ABS Royalex has more design flexibility, and lacks some of the annoying characteristics of metal. A more recent entry into the materials derby is polyethylene (trade name Ram–X). It has the attraction of low price and durability, but it is subject to design limitations due to its inability to hold a shape without a supporting superstructure.

PADDLES

The shape of the paddle blade and grip really make little difference, which is probably why there are so many variations. The length of the paddle, its weight and ability to withstand abuse are something else again. The paddle should be as tall as your shoulders, or no higher than your eyes, and generally the stern paddler will prefer the longer length, the bow paddler, the shorter. You should carry one extra, full-sized paddle in each canoe, and be sure to provide a junior-sized one for each kid. It may spend most

Wood paddles: four examples of laminated paddles flanked by traditional ash paddles. Note the varieties of grips—all are satisfactory. Laminated blades are covered with a layer of fiberglass for added durability; two have fiberglass tips for protection.

of its time in the bottom of the canoe, but you will be amazed at the contribution kid-power can make when they do decide to put them to work (notice—they decide, not you).

Paddles may be of wood or synthetic materials. It is increasingly difficult to find a good quality, solid ash, maple, or spruce canoe paddle, but there are a number of handsome, laminated wood paddles on the market. We are not referring to the "popsicle sticks" kept in barrels in sporting goods stores or motorboat stores (although a small version of these would be satisfactory for the kids), but to those designed for serious canoers. Woods that might otherwise be too soft or light are strengthened by multiple laminations, or with a thin layer of fiberglassing. This further enables the manufacturer to offer a shaft with comfortable flex and a thinly profiled blade. The best wood paddles are likely to be more expensive than comparable synthetics, but will be more aesthetically appealing.

Synthetic paddles come in more different shapes and

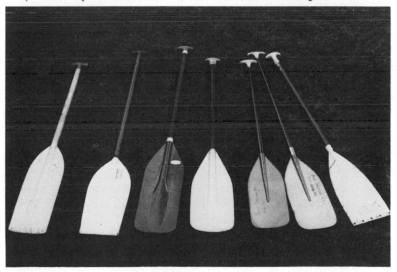

Synthetic paddles: **left to right**—Norse, Seda, Blue Hole, Iliad, Old Town (experimental featherweight), Old Town (same), Nona. The stiffer, heavier ones are more appropriate for whitewater. The recreational paddler and canoe tripper will be looking for a lighter paddle with some flex in the shaft.

combinations of materials than one can imagine, but look for one that is light, with perhaps an epoxy blade, and a polyester handle (like a fiberglass fishing pole), which will be more "giving" than an aluminum shaft. Light weight and some "give" in the shaft will tend to be less wearing on a canoe tripping paddler, and if you multiply the number of likely paddle strokes per minute times the likely number of hours spent paddling, the logic of choosing a light paddle is readily seen.

LIFE JACKETS

They have now been born again as PFDs (Personal Flotation Devices). In addition to being safe and sane—especially where kids are involved—they are also the law. The Coast Guard–approved Type III PFD design has been designated as *de rigueur* for canoeists. Based on our research, that seems to mean a life jacket that will not necessarily support an unconscious victim face up (Type I), but does offer a sufficient compromise between buoyancy and comfort to encourage people to wear it.

The PFD manufacturers have caught on to fashion, so now the lowly life preserver is served up in snappy styles and colors; perhaps a denim. And you can choose from some evocative names, such as the 'Deliverance' or the 'Gran Sport 505'. Besides adding a dash of color to your canoeing wardrobe, PFDs provide a cushion for your kid's back, or a cushion for camp (a use which may also shorten their life). Under a windbreaker or rain parka, they can provide warmth.

PFDs come in tube or panel designs, and your choice will be a matter of personal preference, although the latter may be somewhat more comfortable and may permit more freedom of motion. PFDs come in different sizes, so check to make sure that there is sufficient flotation for your weight. For the kids, the life vest should not be so large that they might slip out of it in the water.

PFDs are a little like seat belts; you have to get into

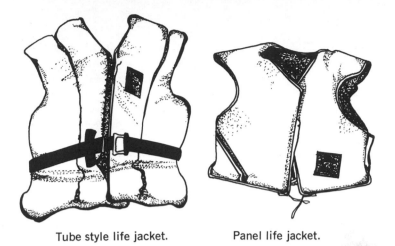

Tube style life jacket.   Panel life jacket.

the habit of putting them on. In days bygone, we were
somewhat lax, unless we were running rapids. But good
sense calls for making the PFD a part of the canoeing
routine; like lacing up your jogging shoes or fastening
your ski safety strap. With the kids along it is an impera-
tive, and it is easy to get them in the habit when they are
young.

PACKS AND PACKING

There are a number of objectives in the packing strategy.
For short trips, or if the only portage will be to and from
the car at the put-in and take out, one can consolidate the
gear in the largest possible packs, with minimal regard
to carrying comfort. On the other hand, if one is contemplating longer trips, requiring frequent making and
breaking of camp, or portaging, a shrewder analysis is
called for.

Frequent loading and unloading, stuffing and un-stuffing,
as well as propinquity to water, sand, and grit require
packs for canoeing which are sturdier than their backpacking counterparts. That means heavier gauge canvas or
nylon, rigid and semi-rigid packs, and ones with simple
closures. Avoid those with lots of vulnerable pouches, com-

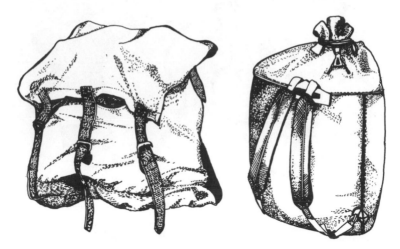

Duluth pack.   Nylon Klamath pack.

partments, stitching and multiple zippers. In fact, most frame-type packs, unless they are specially designed with a short frame, are awkward for canoe camping.

The canoer's traditional workhorse is the Duluth pack; a large canvas envelope with leather straps and tumpline (for the head), lined with double, heavy-gauge garbage or leaf bags, which can be stuffed with clothing, sleeping bags and mats. One Duluth pack should be reserved for "dirty" gear: the tents, tarp, axe, grill, tools, rain gear when not in use (on top where you can get at it), and the wet tennis shoes. These are also good packs for packing food, but be careful not to create a backbreaking monster.

Not as strong—and probably not suitable for carrying food or heavy gear—are Duluth-like bags made of nylon, with their own plastic liner. These packs can be made watertight by means of a drawstring around the top. Much lighter than the canvas packs, they can hold a generous amount of clothing and bedding and are manageable by all but the smallest kids. Kid-power can also be tapped by making up personal packs for each of them, whereby they carry their own clothes, for example. Just make sure

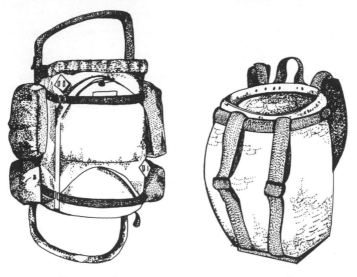

Frame pack.   Pack basket.

that you make provision for keeping it dry. Small garbage
bags may be used for this purpose.

The objective of your packing strategy will be a place
for everything, and everything in its place, so that every
meal or pitching of camp is not a free-for-all. In the case
of crushables, such as certain food items, frequently needed
items, or the makings for lunch, you may want at least
one rigid pack, like a pack basket, fiberglass pack, or
homemade wanigan. The latter is a wooden box with shelf
and tumpline (see Chapter 6, on Food).

Another part of the canocist's packing strategy is to
have gear packed and organized so that it is in units that
are portable within the physical limitations of your crew.
Four jam-packed Duluth packs is a tidy consolidation, but
the achievement is self-defeating if Dad is the only one who
can lift them. Yet, a proliferation of small packs may require
you to make four trips on every portage; if you are able to
keep track of them at all. Finally, you want to be able to
find things when they are needed, and you don't want
to find them wet, broken or crushed.

There is no perfect solution to the packing riddle, and

The traditional Duluth pack with leather straps and tumpline. These can accommodate prodigious loads, reducing the number of trips necessary to cross a portage. Be careful not to make them too heavy, however. If you are going to carry two packs over a short portage, put the second one on top. Don't try to carry it in front or on one arm.

everyone eventually develops his own strategy, one which is likely to change as the composition of the crew changes. One of our family canoeing acquaintances passed an important milestone this summer when their oldest daughter was suddenly able to portage her own canoe. Personal preference is important, too. Some people like boxes, some, bags. Some are perfectly happy with backpacks—frames, zippers, pouches and all, plus a loop for the ice axe.

Canoe tripping with kids

A waterproof "Dry Box" is great if portages are few, or short. Note also the temporary seat just ahead of the center thwart, so that one of the junior passengers can paddle comfortably.

They're probably okay too, especially if that's what you've got in your closet!

TENTS

Treat yourself to the largest tent you can justify, consistent with weight. This does not mean a circus tent with a tinker-toy frame; but there are available some good-sized tents permitting you to stand up—or almost—made of rip-stop nylon, and usually provided with a separate rain fly. Whether you have young kids in the same tent with you, or whether they have their own tent, they tend to be active, both awake and asleep, and the more room they have, the better—particularly if it rains. There is no need to live in a mole hole.

Having kids along means twice as many entrances and

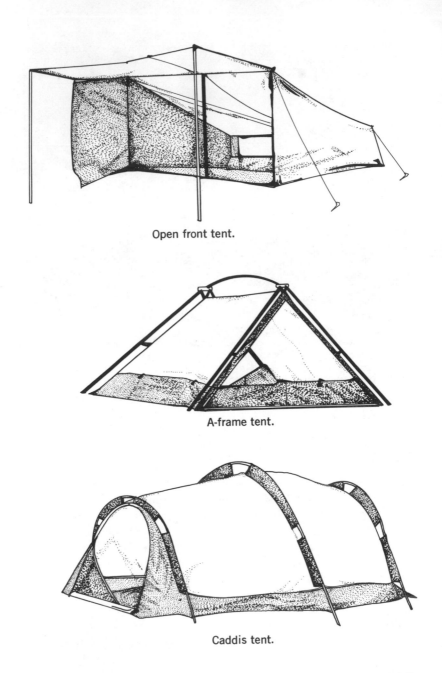

Open front tent.

A-frame tent.

Caddis tent.

Canoe tripping with kids

exits, usually at a high-speed lurch. Zippers get yanked and abused. Little toes and protruding elbows take part of the tent with them, coming and going. Each arrival brings a new load of forest duff. All of which suggests that you are going to need a bigger tent, and a well-made tent. We have been able to get along nicely for many years with some very simple designs, so it is not necessary to pay a king's ransom for fancy features aimed at backpackers and would-be mountaineers. Simple A frames, miner's tents, semi-wall tents, or Baker tents are good canoeing shelter. If you are willing to spend more money, the Draw Tite style of tent is an excellent choice. In the past, we have bought moderately priced wall tents, and made our own rain fly from coated nylon and an inexpensive grommet kit available in most camping stores.

One of the main reasons we stress size in selecting a tent is that larger often means drier; less likelihood of acrobatic young sleepers ending up against the tent wall, and less claustrophobia in the case of a forced incarceration. That goes for Mom and Dad, too. Larger floor space also means there are more places to escape from the puddles that collect even in the best of tents, due to pitching on uneven ground, strong winds, or just a prolonged downpour.

We deal more with the subject of staying dry in another chapter, so perhaps you should turn your thoughts to the sunny skies and gentle breezes that are likely to accompany your canoe trips. In good weather as well as bad you will want a tent that can be ventilated. Sitting in the sun, the tent can get incredibly hot. A light color and ample vents help. The lighter colored tents have the added attraction of being a cheerier abode, permitting you to do your diary in the morning and to read in your tent at night without candles or flashlights.

SLEEPING BAGS AND MATS

There is nothing as comfortable as an air mat, and nothing as exasperating as one which springs a leak in the middle of the night. The inexpensive ones are too prone to puncture. The tough ones are heavy, and it is a chore to completely deflate them when you are trying to break camp. There have been some recent innovations, such as the Air Lift mattress, lightweight, compartmentalized nylon envelopes, and separate plastic tubes (with extras), and the self-inflating Therma–Rest mat. The latter combines the comfort of air with the convenience and warmth of a mat.

We wouldn't spend a fortune on mats for the littlest kids. It is desirable to have them off the ground, but they seem absolutely incapable of staying on any kind of mat. Unlike you and me, they also seem to be totally oblivious to hard ground, or even roots and rocks, being perfectly content to curl up around the little lumps and prods that would keep grownups awake all night.

Half-, or three-quarter length foam mats, in a light nylon shell, which can be compressed into a tight little roll, will do fine for the kids. The older members of the crew may want something a little more substantial. One manufacturer has cleverly bonded an open-celled foam to a thinner sheet of closed-cell foam, seemingly on the same principle as the running shoes in which one sole lamination is for comfort, and the other for protection against pebbles and hard surfaces. We have had good luck with mats in this design called Pak–Foam.

Although the adults may want to treat themselves to a fine sleeping bag, it is not necessary to spend a fortune on bags for the kids. Kids seem to sleep warmer and be less concerned about the size or cut of the bag than the parents. This is true well into their teens, so we would suggest buying junior-sized bags and being willing to go with a "mummy" shape. In both cases, you will be cutting down on weight, and the tighter fit of the smaller mummy shape will compensate for any deficiency of its being a sewn-through bag (a satisfactory but less expensive method of construction than offset or baffle-type bags) in terms of providing warmth. We bought two inexpensive, junior-sized down bags from a very reputable manufacturer, and after giving almost eight year's service to our own kids, they have been on frequent loan to friends, for their juniors, to this very day.

Since we purchased those sleeping bags, some new fillings have come on the market. In the meantime, the price of down-filled bags has escalated mercilessly. Today, you can buy bags filled with Polargard or Fiberfil II insulating (at considerably less cost than comparably cut bags in down), made by several of the manufacturers who have already established their reputation with down. These bags are not quite as compressible as down bags, but can be stuffed (rather than rolled up) like down, and have the added advantage of being able to provide warmth even when wet. This is a major advantage for kids, in whom the careless factor runs high, or if occasional bed wetting is a problem.

Whether your bag is filled with down or one of the new synthetics, a lot of care should be taken in the packing of the sleeping bag to ensure its dryness. A wet sleeping bag is a genuine drag! Some of the stuff bags have a water-resistant material such as coated nylon, but many do not. In either case, they often are in the bottom of the pack, which happens to sit on the floor of the canoe, soaking up water like a wick all day from the famous, inevitable puddle. This is another good reason for lining with plastic the packs which will contain your bedding and clothing.

TOOLS AND OTHER EQUIPMENT

We deal with some of the other gear, including clothing and kitchen utensils, in another chapter, but it may be worthwhile to discuss some of the nonessentials. Of course, one man's or woman's nonessentials are another's can't-do-withouts. We have often touted the relative comfort in which the canoe tripper can live—compared to some of his self-propelled counterparts—but there is still a point at which the decision must be made: "Do I want to lug this to and from the canoes, across the portages, and risk losing track of an ungainly inventory of gew-gaws, or is it something that will truly enhance our comfort and enjoyment of the trip?"

Binoculars are an example of one of those extras which seem like a good idea but never leave the pack; yet, if one of your primary purposes for the trip is birdwatching, they're a must. An ice chest may be fine for a day trip, or one which will employ the base-camp approach (see Chapter 10, Underway), but for most canoe trips it is an awkward companion, inviting additional weight. We almost never carry a flashlight, much less a lantern, but a couple of disposable penlights may be useful for poking around in the tent after dark for stray bits of kid-strewn gear. In the woods, it is surprising how well your eyes adjust to darkness, and it stays light quite late during most of the popular summer canoe tripping months. Large flashlights or lanterns seem out of keeping with the natural environment, and as often as not create more blind spots than illumination, especially when you happen to stumble with unadjusted pupils out of the area of direct light.

If open fires are permitted, and wood is ample, why carry a stove? For a rainy day, you say. Perhaps, but you are presented with many of the same problems on that kind of day, in getting your stove started, as you are in starting a fire. For the other five days you are carrying around extra weight and fuel, which invariably ends up permeating everything within seventeen feet of it. Unless I use a stove regularly, it usually takes me an hour to figure how to start the darn thing, anyway. The propane variety seems simplest, but they don't give off much heat in relation to their bulk. Nonetheless, we often take a small stove. Usually it gets used once. Suit yourself.

If you are going to have a fire, take a folding saw for cutting wood to length, and a small Hudson's Bay axe (no hatchets please, particularly with kids around) for splitting. Matches—preferably waterproofed, wooden ones—in a waterproof match case, should be carried in a secure, available place. If wet weather is a threat, there are commercial fire-starters in tablet or tube form, or you can use a common table candle. The latter also comes in handy for illumination, but not in the tent.

I like to carry a small sheath knife for cutting rope, feathering sticks to start the fire, cleaning fish, tightening screws, sharpening marshmallow toasters, and a host of other glamorous chores. You'll need a sharpening stone, for both the knife and the axe, and in the case of the latter, I prefer a round stone. A small file is even better for axe-sharpening, and after you have put an edge on with the file, the stone can be used to finish it off.

The file and the sharpening stone are part of my tool kit, which I carry in a screw-topped plastic jar. Here, undoubtedly, is the part of the gear list where I have gone out of control. To me the additional weight of the tool kit is worth the satisfaction of knowing that there is no emergency or repair for which I am not prepared, and I lord it over other less fortunate members of the trip who must beg me for one of the kit's rare components. Here are some of its coveted items as recalled from a recent family canoe trip:

Miniature pliers and wrench
Nesting screwdriver
Waterproof matches
Snaps and plastic grommets
Assorted screws and nails
Electrical tape
Small can opener
Tube of airplane cement (a very hot item with some of the junior craftsmen on the trip)
Three-In-One oil
Assorted needles and thread, plus thimble!
Rubber bands

Many of the contents of this "survival" kit never see the light of day, but the fun of assembling the contents and knowing they are there is as important as the practical need. Someone out there with a nice big flashlight wonders why I can't get along without a roll of electrical tape and a pocket knife.

There follows a more traditional checklist of gear:

Canoe Equipment
16½- to 18½-foot canoes.
Paddles (one extra per canoe).
PFDs (life preservers for each person).
Lines for bow and stern (heavy sash cord or nylon).
Carrying yoke.
Duct tape for repairs.
Sponge or bailer (the latter can be fashioned from an empty plastic Clorox bottle).

Camp Gear
Tent(s).
Rain fly for tent, and tarp for use as ground cloth or additional rain shelter.
Axe and saw.
Rope and more rope. (No matter how much we take, it all gets used. Take several different sizes of sash cord and nylon parachute-type line. One of our companions built his wife a chaise longue, using tree branches and four hanks of sash cord, during one of our more languid rest days.)

Bedding
Sleeping bags.
Mats.
Water-resistant stuff bags. (Will serve as a pillow with the day's clothing stuffed in them at night.)

Packs
Canvas Duluth packs.
Nylon Duluth-type pack.
Duffle bag.

Personal or ruck sacks for kids.

Waterproof bag or box for sensitive gear such as camera.

Pack basket, fiberglass pack or wooden wanigan for some food and "crushable" items.

Heavy-duty garbage or leaf bags; heavy rubber bands for closures.

Waterproof bags or Dry Box® if nature of trip calls for extreme security, and/or weight is not a critical factor.

Miscellaneous
Compass
Suntan lotion or sunscreen.
Insect repellent.
Diaries.
Toilet paper.
Tool and repair kit.

Chapters 5 and 6 on Clothing, Food, and Kitchen contain appropriate lists for those parts of the outfit.

5: Clothing

He was dressed in shirt of doeskin,
White and soft, and fringed with ermine,
All inwrought with beads of wampum;
He was dressed in deer-skin leggings,
Fringed with hedgehog quills and ermine,
And in moccasins of buck-skin,
Thick with quills and beads embroidered.

In clothing both yourself and the children for a canoe trip, it is important to dress in a manner which will prepare everyone for the range of weather conditions that may be encountered. One should know the general climate of the area and choose comfortable, appropriate clothing. Clothing is as critical as your food, and can mean the difference between a miserable experience or a wonderful adventure.

Since canoe trippers, like backpackers, need to "watch their weight," the trick is to meet all the clothing needs without sinking the canoes to the gunwales. As it turns out, kids probably need a greater assortment of clothes than woodswise adults, for several reasons. They are likely to get dirtier, wetter and colder (or warmer) than their adult counterparts. They tend not to pay attention to staying dry or clean, and are less adept than adults in regulating their own body thermostats.

There are no big-name brands in canoe clothing, as there are, for instance, in ski clothing; and there is really no need to spend a lot of money on the children's gear. In fact, your children probably have ample clothing in their closets right now. As one becomes more familiar with canoeing, however, it makes sense to add items to the wardrobe that can be used for canoeing as well as other outdoor activities.

Even if you decide on the economy route, it is still great fun to browse through the catalogues of companies specializing in new outdoor equipment. The Eddie Bauer and L. L. Bean catalogues are eagerly awaited and well-dog-eared prizes in our household. At the end of the chapter is a list of mail order suppliers, most of whom have a good selection of lightweight, easy-to-use, trouble-saving equipment, with prices ranging as widely as the variety of merchandise.

DRESSING IN LAYERS

To keep the canoeing outfit as light as possible, one should dress using the "layering system." Dress the children in an inner layer of loosely knit material which goes next to the skin. In the summer, this might be a cotton T-shirt and underpants. In the winter, fishnet or wool underwear may be called for. For protection from the cold, the object is to trap the body heat next to the body, while in hot weather the idea is for the bottom layer to absorb perspiration. The second layer is the insulating layer, and can change depending on the climate and the weather. In the summer, it may not be necessary to wear more than one shirt of lightweight cotton. In colder weather several shirts, and a sweater may be required—shortsleeved, longsleeved, cotton and wool. The final layer is the outer protecting layer, which may be a windbreaker, sweatshirt, parka or rain gear. They all might be appropriate depending on the climate and the season. Wool is strongly recommended for cold-weather canoeing because it takes longer to absorb moisture and retains body heat even when wet. The layers of clothing can be stripped away as the day warms up, and added as the sun goes down.

The nature of the activity for which you dress is also important. What may be proper and comfortable for the adults is not always appropriate for small children. If Mom and Dad are paddling on a cold, rainy day and the kids are sitting amidships counting pine trees, they are going to be cold! Paddling is an exercise that can really warm you up. Take into consideration the activities of everyone in the group and add a layer or two for the inactive members.

How much clothing one should take for children will depend on the climate, the season and the length of time the group will be out. In selecting the clothes for the little ones, it makes sense to have at least two changes, but the general rule is, the younger they are, the more changes required. By the time they are teenagers, just one complete change with additional underwear and socks will do.

Bright colors tend to absorb heat and make one feel warmer on a hot day, and, according to the old-timers, are more attractive to mosquitoes and black flies. With protection in mind, long sleeves and long pants shield arms and legs from scratches and insect bites around camp and on the portage.

Pants for canoeists should be made of a sturdy material; denim and corduroy are fine but they don't dry very quickly. Bell bottoms have a nasty way of inviting hungry insects to explore the lower limbs, so we have found that straight-leg cotton or a synthetic blend are best. Tucked into the socks, they are neat, and discourage nosy, unwanted bugs. The cotton or blends also dry quickly.

The outer clothing layer should be wind and water repellent. This could be a sweatshirt, a parka, a windbreaker or a rainsuit. As down and cotton do not retain body heat when wet, they may not be a good choice for this layer unless worn under a rainsuit or poncho. Nothing will be served if the child is so bundled up that he can't move, so try to keep the bulk to a minimum, while, at the same time, providing warmth.

Cold feet? Try the layering system again! Bottom layer of light cotton or nylon with woolen socks on top; then the boot or shoe. It is particularly important to keep all of the juniors' boots and shoes well waterproofed. Wet feet quickly become cold feet. Aside from constant vigilance on the part of the parents, waterproofing, rubbers or a plastic bag over the foot, inside the boot or shoe are the best safeguards against wet, cold feet. Our son spent a wonderful vacation fishing with his grandfather in Labrador, but the trip was somewhat marred each evening because David always had wet feet. They went unnoticed while he was fishing but became unbearably cold when he stopped.

It could also be that when your child complains of cold feet, he needs a hat. Cold feet may experience a miraculous warming up when a wool hat is used as a lid, since the head and neck radiate about 25 percent of the body's heat.

FOOTWEAR

For boots and shoes, nothing but the toughest will suffice. We strongly recommend the kind with leather uppers and rubber bottoms, such as the L. L. Bean Maine Hunting Shoe. Boots are invaluable on the portages, as they help to keep the kids' feet warm and dry, and provide a good support for the ankles. Around camp, a pair of sneakers is satisfactory. When having the kids' boots fitted, the boots should be tried on over two pairs of socks, so the toes will have enough room on a cold morning. On the other hand, they should not be too big, as slipping and sliding inside the boot causes blisters. Another cause of blisters are those socks that keep disappearing into the boot. Knee socks tend to stay up more dependably on short stocky legs. Children need to break in their boots just as adults do. Wearing their boots around the house can be part of the pre-trip psych-up.

RAIN GEAR

The most important item of clothing for kids is their rain gear. If a child is cold and wet, it goes without saying that the parents are going to be miserable, too. This is one area where you get what you pay for. Be prepared to pay a little more to obtain the very best rain gear that can be found.

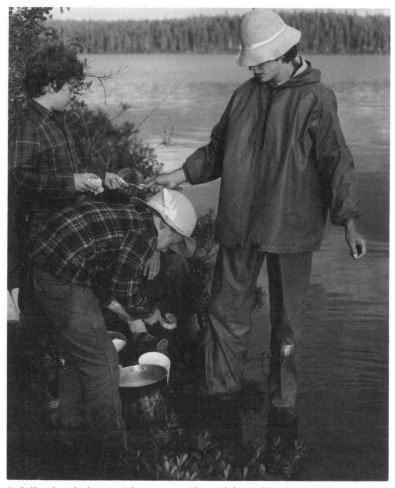

A full rainsuit is good insurance. (See Living with the Inevitable, page 157.) Getting kids to pitch in on the camp chores is one of the rewards of canoeing with kids.

Ponchos are an old standby, and they are certainly appealing when price and simplicity are considered. They will envelop a person, even with a pack on, and find many uses as tarp, shelter, ground cloth and covering for gear on a rainy night. If a poncho is your choice for rain gear, here are some suggestions: A hood provides built-in protection against rivulets down the neck; strong positive snaps ensure the poncho won't blow open under the stress of paddling or other activities. Our chief objection to the poncho is its activity-inhibiting qualities. It is also a danger around the campfire, as it billows out from the wearer. That problem is easily solved, however, by a piece of rope or a belt around the midsection.

Our own choice is for a full rainsuit, but good ones are expensive. It's no fun trying to carry a pack across a portage with your rain pants falling down. Make sure the pants have a durable waist fastener or drawstring. Velcro, snaps or elastic cuffs will do the job, and should hold up under a child's normal abuse. The jacket should have a hood and be large enough to accommodate all those clothing layers, while allowing enough room for air to circulate. This is necessary to prevent condensation on the inside.

HATS

Hats, lids and bonnets will keep the rain and the sun off little heads and out of the eyes. The hats can be worn under the hood of the rain jacket to keep the rain from pelting into young faces. There are an infinite variety of hats, but some make more sense than others. A brim may be an important consideration, but perhaps the best bet is to let the kids choose their own style. Our son favors a battered old felt hat that resembles the one his father has worn for many years. Our daughters have worn almost everything, from a sailor hat with the brim turned down to the felt-crushable pocket variety. Mom favors a stetson. The hat is not only a functional piece of clothing, but a personality piece. Here is an opportunity to let the kids express their individualities.

Your family will very likely already have most of the clothing needed for a canoe trip. The very desirable woolen items can be expensive, and everyone seems to outgrow them before the first button pops off. Therefore you'll probably have to do some shopping. There are several ways to cut the cost of good woolen outdoor wear. Woolen underwear and shirts and sweaters can be found at ski exchanges, the Salvation Army, Goodwill Industries, and other secondhand shops. These clothes seldom wear out, and can be handed down within the family. A moth-eaten wool sweater or shirt, too grubby even for suburban chores, can be mended to provide a very functional and woods-compatible garment. Another find at the ski exchanges are the unlined warm-up pants. These are usually water repellent, and can be adapted as the bottoms to a rainsuit.

Once you set your imagination to work, there are lots of ways to cut the costs on the specialty items, and still be warm, dry and appropriately dressed.

CLOTHES FOR KIDS

6 Pair underwear (number depending on age and reliability of child for staying dry).
6 Pair socks (kneesocks, wool, cotton and nylon).
2 Long-sleeved pajamas or a footed sleeper.
2 Pair pants.
1 Pair shorts.
2 Short-sleeved shirts.
1 Jacket (windbreaker-parka).
1 Rainsuit (shirt should fit below the waist—pants adjusted to height).
1 Pair boots (above the ankle)
1 Pair sneakers (might want to include a pair of rubbers).
1 Hat.
2 Bandana.

Canoe tripping with kids

CATALOGUES

Eastern Mountain Sports, Inc.
12312 Vose Farm Road
Peterborough, New Hampshire 03458

Frostline Kits
Dept. WCA18
Frostline Circle
Denver, Colorado 80241

Early Winters, Ltd.
110 Prefontaine Place South
Seattle, Washington 98104

Recreational Equipment Inc.
P.O. Box c-88125
Seattle, Washington 98188

L. L. Bean, Inc.
Freeport, Maine 04033

Country Ways (Kits)
3500 Highway 101 South
Minnetonka, Minnesota 55343

Holubar Mountaineering Ltd.
P.O. Box 7, Dept. 141A12
1975 30th Street
Boulder, Colorado 80306

Eddie Bauer
Dept. EWC
15th & Union
Seattle, Washington 98124

Moor and Mountain
Dept. 57
63 Park Street
Andover, Massachusetts 01810

6: Food

First they ate the sturgeon, Nahma,
And the pike, the Maskenozha,
Caught and cooked by old Nokomis;
Then on pemican they feasted,
Pemican and buffalo marrow,
Haunch of deer and hump of bison,
Yellow cakes of the Mondamin,
And the wild rice of the river.

Kids love to eat. In planning the food for any excursion, a weekend or a month-long voyage, remember that kids love to eat! To make life easiest for all, why not plan your menus around their likes? Meals are no fun for anyone when you have to coax picky eaters. In the early days of trail foods, our kids could not be induced to swallow any of the dried eggs (and who could blame them?). The answer was to bring along our own variety packs of their favorite mini-boxes of dry cereal. It was certainly quieter and more peaceful to have them enjoying their own personalized breakfasts. Freeze-dried eggs have indeed improved in flavor and texture since those early days, and if the eggs are laced with cheese or bacon bits, you may even get your children to eat them.

Determining the kind of food you carry on your canoe trip will depend on the length of time and the terrain to be covered. For weekends and short trips anything goes; an ice chest full of steaks and hot dogs, or a Spartan diet of dried fruit and nuts. In preparation for a short trip, solicit the kids for ideas on the meals that they would prefer. This

Plan the meals around their "likes." But you can't win them all!
Bowls are preferable to plates. They keep food warmer and there
is less chance of it sliding off.

bit of democracy should make them feel more a part of the
plans, and it certainly is helpful to you on the trip if you
are carrying food you know they will enjoy.

FOOD AS FUEL

Food for canoeing should taste good, look appetizing and
provide plenty of energy for paddling. What works at
home will work in the wilds—except you need more
calories—4000 or more per day if you are working hard.
By comparison, a typical homemaker expends about 1400
calories a day; an office worker, about 2500, and a factory
worker, approximately 3000 calories. An average canoeist
will burn about 5 calories per minute, or 300 calories per
hour.

Carbohydrates provide quick energy and should supply
at least 50 percent of your daily calorie requirement. Fats
contain about twice as many calories per pound as carbohy-

drates, and are the body's major source of stored energy. Fats should provide 20 percent of your daily intake of calories, and for a tough trip this amount should be increased substantially.

Proteins are essential for cell repair (building muscle), but are an inefficient source of calories. The American diet tends to be protein rich, so even without thinking about it, your menu will probably contain an adequate amount.

Your best source of carbohydrate (or "glue" as we sometimes refer to it) will be breads, potatoes, pancakes, rice and hot cereals such as oatmeal. Fortunately, these are all readily available in powdered, or instant form, at the supermarket. Carbohydrates are inexpensive, as well.

For our canoe trips, we have obtained our fats from bacon (canned or slab), salamis or summer sausage, and from whole cheeses. Nuts, including peanut butter, are a source of fat, too. Not only does fat provide energy, but we learn from the arctic explorers that it provides a sense of well-being. It is also a lubricant which helps prevent dried hands and chapped lips from prolonged exposure to sun, wind, and water.

There are many tempting and innovative freeze-dried and dehydrated foods especially prepared for the camper, but such fare is often quite expensive and lacks the energy content to keep everyone running efficiently. We recommend building your basic menu of fats and carbohydrates from the supermarket shelf, and then rounding out your menus with some of the interesting meals available from the specialized manufacturers.

PLANNING AND PACKING

When planning your menus it is best to plan and pack by the meal; so many days of breakfasts, lunches and dinners. Then comes an excursion to the local grocery store to buy the essentials. Include the kids, for it will generate enthusiasm for the coming adventure. They will be a part of the effort as they help select the candies for the portages and the marshmallows for the campfire. Upon the return home, spread all the food on your dining room or ping-pong table. You can pack from there by setting the food out in groups of three meals for each day, where you will be able to see exactly what you have, and, more importantly, what you have forgotten!

The grocery store carries virtually all the food necessary for a short trip; everything including canned bacon, instant milk, oatmeal, dried fruit, canned fruit, soups, packaged dinners, and your child's favorite spaghetti and sauce. To reduce both weight and potential trail litter—you must carry out all the packages, wrappers, etc., that you carry in—you should repackage as much of the food as possible. Here again, the kids can assist as the Tang, oatmeal, or sugar is transferred from bottles or boxes into double or triple plastic sandwich bags, secured at the top with twisted rubber bands and labeled for the trail.

For a longer trip requiring less weight, you may want to consider ordering your freeze-dried or dehydrated food by mail. Be sure to order well in advance of your departure date. There are a number of reliable brands to choose from by mail order, with several companies putting out catalogues containing a comprehensive selection for every palate. It may be worth the extra expense to stay with the meat, potatoes and vegetable diet they may be familiar with at home; but consider "one-pot" meals as a necessity for those times when weather, fatigue, fire or stove limitations dictate a short cut. There are going to be some evenings when nobody feels up to a full-scale dinner production.

We have found that by ordering in quantity and repacking the food in single-meal units, we can substantially lower per-serving costs. There are a number of companies which supply freeze-dried fare in Number 10 cans. The price is shocking in any event, but not as atrocious as the one-meal-sized packages. If the itinerary calls for just a few light-weight meals, or to round out your supplies for a long weekend, the local sporting goods store can probably supply your needs.

Part of the meal preparation, and some of the fun, for the canoe trip can begin during the winter months. The woodworkers in the family can design and construct the *wanigan:* a wooden box with tumpline or carrying straps, proportioned to fit between the canoe's gunwales, and with capacity for all the kitchen utensils, plus condiments, the crushable or breakable items, lunch for the coming day, and the tool kit. The seamstress can quickly sew up the cotton or nylon cloth bags in which individual meals or classes of foodstuffs can be placed.

To pack your grub—be organized. The challenge is to eliminate the head-in-the-pack approach to menu planning. This calls for packing each meal in its own cloth bag and labeling it with a Magic Marker. If there is more than one boat in your party, it's a good idea to divide the food evenly between the boats, with so many days' food in each boat. Not only does this ensure that the weight of the heavier food packs gets equitably distributed, but in the unlikely case of an upset, all is not lost. After one rainy, two-week trip with soggy food packs, we resolved that a plastic liner for the Duluth pack is a must

The wanigan.

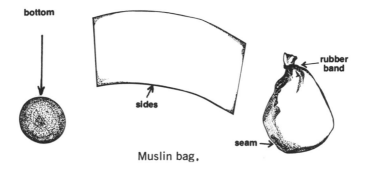

rubber band

sides

seam →

Muslin bag.

for keeping food dry. This liner can be either a garbage bag (heavy duty or a double) or one of the new White-water bags designed for the purpose.

We recommend a special pack in which to carry all the essentials for meal preparation. A rigid pack is a good choice, as is the wanigan described earlier. Ideally, it should have a shelf or the equivalent. Into this pack go matches, stove and/or grill, cutlery set (knives, forks and spoons should be counted after every meal) and nesting pots with detachable handles, frying pans, pots, plates, cups; all fitting together in a sturdy, well-made set. Plastic, not metal, cups are urged, since they keep their contents warm longer, and will not cook a hand or finger after being freshly filled with boiling coffee or soup, as metal cups will. A word about plates versus bowls—for a small child eating without a table, a bowl is much easier to handle—the spaghetti, for example, is less likely to end up slipping off onto the ground. The same comments concerning plastic and metal cups apply here, as well.

Other constituents of the kitchen pack would be aluminum foil, paper towels, toilet paper, dish soap, Pam, SOS, long-handled spoon, hot pads (mitts), seasonings, and most important of all, the next meal. Following each meal, by setting aside in your kitchen pack the next morning's breakfast or the noon meal, with the kids responsible for choosing the menu, you have just saved yourself one more head-in-the-pack session.

PREPARATION

How should one prepare the food so that everyone looks forward to mealtime? The problems are the same as at home, but you do gain advantage when the out-of-doors and uncommon exertion intensify young appetites. In preparing trail foods, we have found the flavors to be somewhat bland and uniform, although they have improved tremendously in the past few years. Consequently, we carry many seasonings: onion flakes, bell peppers, seasoning salt, parsley, curry powder, cinnamon (to spice up rolls), tarragon, bouillon cubes, salt and pepper. In fact, you can bring the same seasonings you use at home. Try it in the woods; you'll like the results. If you want to repackage the spices, use small plastic bags, and label them. A couple of other tips are worth mentioning. We always take Bisquick, which can be used to make dumplings. These are a welcome addition to a too-runny, one-pot meal; moreover, biscuits and dumplings are favorites of the younger set, and are bound to sell well around the campfire.

The kids' outdoor appetites will astound you.

Get them involved in the preparation—like mixing up the biscuit batter.

Blueberry Shortcake

You haven't lived until you have sampled a blueberry shortcake. Have the kids pick five or six cups of berries; mix with the berries a cup of sugar, three or four tablespoons of flour, a pinch of salt and three or four tablespoons of butter or margarine. Add about a quarter cup of water and bring to a boil. Cook it until thickened, and serve over shortcakes made from Bisquick—the recipe for shortcake is on the box. This is guaranteed to send the kids back to the bushes berry-picking in a hurry. Mix a handful of berries in your Bisquick dough or pancake batter, and you have blueberry muffins or pancakes. These are simple chores for the kids to perform, while spicing up the whole menu.

Camped on a creek in the Yukon, we discovered in the shadow of a dilapidated cabin an overgrown garden plot that was still sprouting raspberries and rhubarb—obviously some Klondike Ninety-eighter's much-beloved kitchen garden gone wild. Our kids went to work and ended up producing raspberries for dessert, raspberry syrup for breakfast pancakes, and would you believe, rhubarb pie!

Bannock

Over the years, we must have donated several hundred loaves of bread to camp thieves, such as chipmunks, squirrels, and raccoons. These skillful bandits strike at night, or when camp is unattended, and specialize in liberating well-hidden, locked-up bread. We have tried all kinds of boxes and devices with varying success. One solution has been to bake our bread, more properly "bannock," when we need it, rather than having a supply on hand. This is not that difficult a task, and it is one that can be turned over to an older child. The bread ingredients are all pre-mixed and measured at home and packaged in plastic bags. There are as many recipes for bannock as there are outdoorsmen. Ours calls for one cup of flour to one-half teaspoon baking powder, to one-half cup water and a pinch of salt.

Your designated bread-maker can be in charge of this project from the kitchen to the campfire. At your camp or lunch site, water is added to the ingredients right in the plastic bag to make a kneadable blob, and spread in a frying pan, which has been greased and warmed over the fire. Do not make the dough much over an inch thick, as it tends to burn before cooking through. Now the little old bread-maker can place the skillet over a moderate fire until

Examining the bannock—kitchen complete with rain fly and a good supply of dry firewood.

The biscuits cook in the reflector oven at the same time the main dish is prepared. Gravy and seasonings are off the supermarket shelf.

the bottom is crusted and lightly brown, after which the dough can be flipped over and browned on the other side or the entire pan propped up against a stone to face the fire. Your bannock can also be cooked in a reflector oven,* which, as the name implies, is a device for reflecting heat from the campfire evenly toward both the top and bottom of the pan of food being baked. With a good fire going, you can regulate the temperature by moving the oven toward the heat or further away from it. When used

* A recent check of several purveyors of outdoor gear uncovered no reflector ovens suggesting that they may face extinction.

properly, the reflector oven can do a surprisingly first-class job of baking pies, cakes, biscuits, and casseroles.

Gorp

Another mix-ahead is gorp—with as many recipes as there are practitioners of the art—but generally compounded of dried fruit, nuts, granola, M&Ms or the like, and kept handy for snacks in the canoe or on the portage trail. Whether gorp or its equivalent is on your trip bill of fare, you will want to have energizing finger-foods available, either for a between-meal boost or as a temporary meal when the daily schedule becomes unglued for whatever reason.

Stuffed Fish

All aspects of camping should be fun, and the byword is flexibility! This is especially true in cooking. Be inventive and experiment. Let the kids try their hand. I've mentioned some of the excitement of picking out trail snacks, as well as the possibilities in nature's own bounty, such as raspberries or blueberries. If the male or female members of the expedition are fishermen, a whole new vista opens up. The same juniors who will turn their noses up at filet of sole almondine at home will be fighting over freshly caught and fried trout, perch, or walleye, served at any meal. A great crowd-pleaser that calls for a little innovation is baked stuffed fish. This should be a good-sized lake trout, pike, or other large food fish. The fish is opened down the belly, cleaned and stuffed with whatever ingredients you have on hand. I have successfully used crumbled bannock, gorp, onion flakes, seasoning salt, and dried parsley. The outside of the finny one, brushed with margarine and wrapped in aluminum foil, is buried in the coals at the back of the fire and cooked until it flakes. Served with homemade biscuits, beans and home-fries, you have a meal fit for kid or king.

As night settles in, you're going to have to offer a substitute for the marvels of that most pervasive of all home entertainers—the television. We would submit that marshmallows and popcorn over a dwindling campfire can provide tremendous psychic, if not physical, nourishment, and are probably more beneficial on all counts than the tube.

Smores

Another star in the trail-foods-for-kids galaxy is *Smores*, a concoction of graham crackers, marshmallows and Hershey bars, baked near the fire until a gooey fusion occurs. This unappetizing (to adults) confection will unfailingly call forth sybaritic cries of "give me *s'more*." There is a time and a place for everything. We're all in favor of natural and nutritious meals, especially when there is a day's work to be done, but don't forget when you get back to nature, those occasional sinful indulgences are a pittance in a far more wholesome way of life than is pursued during the other fifty weeks a year.

THE COOKING FIRE

And speaking of sin, we're well aware of the fire-building problem—too many canoers and campers, and a dwindling supply of dead, usable wood. Assuming you may be fortunate enough to travel a waterway where fires are permitted, however, and assuming that necessary ingredients are available, we feel we must make comment on the canoe camper's best friend. Fire-building can be everyone's job, or a special task reserved for the super fire-builder. Small children can be mobilized as the kindling-gatherers. They can be instructed how to hunt out dry wood by checking the lower branches of many types of evergreens, which are usually dead, but are well protected and dry even on the wettest of days. These branches also break off easily and are convenient to gather. In dry weather there is usually tinder and kindling lying about on the ground waiting to be harvested by little hands. The veteran woodsmen refer to this as "squaw wood," but so long as it is convenient and combustible, you can ignore this belittlement. In wet weather or dry, be sure to gather enough wood for the next meal (or several), and keep it dry under a pack or tarp.

The fire for cooking should be very small and hot, and placed to avoid the wind. You may need to construct a windbreak of stones. During our trips to the arctic barrens (appropriately named), we have discovered just how little wood is required for a cooking fire when one is forced to be frugal. Make the fire smaller than you think you will need, and let it burn down a bit before you start to cook. A supply of wood should be on hand before you start to cook, and new wood added a piece at a time, or you will have a bonfire instead of a cookfire. The sides and the back of the fire can be used to keep food hot until serving time.

K.P.*

How do you clean up all this after a meal, and who does it? We all share the duties, taking turns. Mom and one child might take one meal, and Dad and another child, the next. We have discovered that small children are willing workers if an adult works with them, but when asked to do the same job themselves, they are stricken with amnesia and have to be poked and prodded to accomplish the simplest task. Perhaps this time can be used to talk

* Kitchen Police (in case you had forgotten).

Canoe tripping with kids

quietly, getting to know your children better, while you both pitch in with the dirty work.

For general dishwashing, there are two schools of thought. If all campers and canoers were to dump their sudsy water back into the lakes and rivers, the pristine lakes and rivers would soon end up with problems similar to Lake Erie, so you may want to go the "no soap" route. Rinse the dishes in hot water and wipe with paper towels, and if they are really greasy, try burning the grease off over the campfire. Better yet, carry paper plates.

If you use soap—and there are special biodegradable soaps made for campers—try washing the dishes in heated or boiling water to which soap has been added. But instead of pouring out water on the ground or into the lake or river, dig a small hole, lining the bottom with a few rocks, and pour in the water. Then fill the hole back in. Greasy, sudsy water thrown on the ground, besides being unattractive, is a magnet for flies and other unwelcome guests. For the same reason, all litter should be burned, and what won't burn must be packed out. Cans should be washed or burned (no food odor) and then flattened, making them easier to pack out. It's been said before, but we'll say it again: *Take only pictures and memories and leave only footprints.*

Mealtime on the trail, especially the evening meal, should be a time to look forward to; a time to relax and relive the day's adventures. This rewarding scenario can best be accomplished by bringing and preparing only foods the kids will eat willingly. You should stick to your menu as the voyage progresses, by involving everyone in the food selection process at the outset of the trip, the "Yuk" and "Oh, gross" exclamations can be kept to a minimum. The good news is that even if there are some unavoidable miscalculations in the menu, less fussy outdoor appetites tend to take over as the trip unfolds. This will get you off the hook sometimes, but without a doubt, with the kids along, food is the single most important ingredient for a successful trip—so, plan wisely and well.

KITCHEN SUPPLIES AND SAMPLE THREE-DAY MENU

Kitchen Pack

Nesting pots.
Plastic cups.
Plastic bowls (preferable to plates).
2-quart juice container.
Knives, forks, spoons.
Soup ladle and large spoon.
Spatula.
Aluminum foil.
Paper towels, dishtowel or Handi-Wipes.
Reflector oven.
Skillet with collapsible handle.
Scrub pads.
Dish soap (biodegradables are available).
Toilet paper.
Fireplace grill.
Stove and spare parts (priming paste).
Wide-mouth containers.
Spices (salt, pepper, etc.).
Matches.
Firestarters (hexamine tablets or candles).
Extra plastic sandwich bags (Ziploc bags).
Water purification tablets (if necessary).
Griddle.
Goose-neck pliers (makes good pot grabber).

Day One

Breakfast
oatmeal
dried fruit (stewed)
sugar (brown)
Tang
coffee or cocoa

Lunch
cheese and salami
hard crackers or bread
Kool-Aid
soup (instant or bouillon)
tea (milk, sugar)

Dinner
spaghetti
bread
green beans
marshmallows
instant pudding
coffee (milk, sugar)

Day Two

Breakfast
Tang
pancakes (add water only)
bacon (cured, slab)
syrup
coffee (milk, sugar)
cocoa

Lunch
peanut butter and jelly sandwiches
soup
Kool-Aid
tea

Dinner
canned ham (Spam)
potatoes (pre-packaged hash browns)
corn
cocoa
coffee (milk, sugar)
instant pudding
marshmallows

Day Three

Breakfast
   Tang
   hot or cold cereal
   dried fruit (stewed)
   toast
   coffee
   milk

Lunch
   baked beans and franks
   brown bread
   soup
   Kool-Aid
   tea (milk, sugar)

Dinner
   macaroni and cheese (packaged)
   hot dogs (canned sausages)
   peas
   instant pudding
   smores
   cocoa, coffee

WHERE TO WRITE FOR FREE FOOD CATALOGS

Indiana Camp Supply
P.O. Box 344
Pittsboro, Indiana 46167

Mountain House
Dept. Co. Q
Oregon Freeze Dry Foods Inc.
P.O. Box 1048
Albany, Oregon 97321

Stow-A-Way Industries
166 Cushing Highway, Rte. 3A
Cohasset, Massachusetts 02025

7: Wildlife

Then the little Hiawatha,
Learned of every bird its language,
Learned their names and all their secrets,
How they built their nests in summer,
Where they hid themselves in winter. . . .
Of all the beasts he learned the language,
Learned their names and all their secrets,
How the beavers built their lodges,
Where the squirrels hid their acorns . . .
Why the rabbit was so timid . . .

Would-be canoe campers are likely to use animals as an excuse not to try camping. Most often mentioned as the villains are bears and wolves and snakes; beasts purported to regularly dine on small children. In fact, the most dangerous wild creatures the American canoe camper will face are the minute airborne ones; bees, wasps, and hornets, which kill more Americans every year than all the bears, snakes and larger wild creatures combined. Mosquitoes and blackflies may not kill or maim, but they can make for real misery. (In Chapter 12, Living with the Inevitable, we make some suggestions on how to deal with these fellows.)

So much for the "dangerous" wildlife in the canoer's environment, where avoidance is the goal. There is fortunately a whole other world where seeking is the objective. In order to see wildlife in the woods, you have to know how, when, and where to look. With chattering kids along, it is difficult not to announce your presence well in advance of your appearance. The wildlife may well enjoy watching you, but you and your crew will see not a single living creature. On a trip to Labrador, we heard the wolves singing several nights in a row and we looked for them during the day, to no avail. Of course, we made no small amount of noise on the river, and when we put ashore, we could find plenty of tracks indicating that the wolves were following along the shore, undoubtedly watching our progress, and perhaps chuckling to themselves at our crude approach.

SEEING WILDLIFE

With much of the population now living in or near metropolitan areas, it is hard to learn to watch and understand nature. Today's children, raised on Walt Disney nature flicks, or having witnessed animals only in a zoo, are conditioned to expect wild creatures to pose for their pictures, to move slowly, and to perform so all can see. Observing wildlife in its native element is very different. As the canoe approaches you have to have a quick eye to spot a deer slipping through shadows at the edge of the lake, loons diving and resurfacing far out in the lake, or a hawk perched on a rocky ledge.

A good way to train the kids' eyes and ears for a canoe trip is to find a patch of grass—your own lawn, neighborhood, or any local "wilderness"—and have everyone lie on their tummies in the grass. Lying very still and quiet for a few minutes you may then ask, "Who can tell me what they see?" Perhaps it will be an ant carrying a crumb four times its own size; perhaps a blade of grass, a fallen leaf, a flower. Your next question might be, "Can you hear anything?" Again, a few minutes of quiet while all listen, soon taking notice of the wind rustling the leaves, birds singing, a fly buzzing, or a cricket chirping. "Can you feel anything?" A fly crawling across your back, the softness of the grass, the coolness of the ground. "What can you taste?" How does the taste of a blade of grass compare to the taste of a leaf? "Can you smell anything?" It may be the

Canoe tripping with kids

newly cut grass, the damp cool smell of the earth, a flower, and so on. The point is to stimulate their senses and to heighten awareness of the microscopic and oft-times invisible world which comprises the out of doors.

Let's take our new skills and apply them on a canoe trip. While you are preparing for the evening meal or dad is setting up the fishing rods after supper, have the kids sit quietly and try to identify sounds. It won't be long before they are able to recognize the many voices of the wilderness; soon they will become attuned to the evening hooting of the owls, the morning reveille of the crows, the call of the loon, the slap of a beaver's tail in a distant bay; even the drone of millions upon millions of mosquitoes filling the darkening woods, as they snuggle deeper into their sleeping bags, safe from all.

Since we have already determined the futility of group encounters with wildlife, try just a parent and one child, scouting the edges of the lake or river, early in the morning or late in the evening, when the game comes to shore to drink. Practice being quiet. If played like a game, it is a lot of fun to look for the wildlife, and all the troops will want to join in. Status is accorded to the first to spot a forest creature. My father, who accompanies us on many trips, used to offer a "deuce for a moose!" This approach can be carried too far and the point lost, however, as we learned. Our son was returning to camp after an afternoon of fishing, and as he started up the hill to camp he spotted a large black bear standing well above and overlooking our camp. David let out a bellow that could have been heard for miles. "I see a bear; it's a big black one! I saw the bear, *first!*" By that time, the bear was beating a hasty retreat around the hill, into the bushes, and out of sight. The rest of the crew heard only the cries of the sole witness. By the time they clambered out of the tent, Bruno had taken a powder. Since bears are so often cast as the villain, it is curious to note that our visitor, with three delicious Harrisons under his nose, turned and ran at the shrill of young David's voice.

DANGEROUS AND DESTRUCTIVE ANIMALS

What about grizzlies? We were planning a month-long canoe trip in grizzly country, and carried on a lengthy correspondence with our outfitter in Whitehorse in the Yukon. We asked about the advisability of carrying firearms in view of the well-known dangers. A return letter from our distant informant simply counseled us to carry an inexpensive referee's whistle. The whistle alerts bears to your presence before you come upon them, giving them a chance to slip away. It is the grizzly you surprise that is most likely to be a problem.

Bears don't attack humans under normal conditions, but if the bear is looking for food and is in an area where he has been accustomed to finding eatable refuse—usually the legacy of sloppy campers—and you are silly enough to have food in your tent, you just might have a visitor who does not take the trouble to figure out which is people and which is food. If you are canoeing in bear country, put all food in packs and hang well up in a tree, away from the tents, ten feet above the ground and eight feet out from the trunk of the tree. In twenty years of canoeing, often times in well-traveled bear country, we have never had an unwanted intrusion. When it comes to hungry wildlife, the camper will find the raccoons and squirrels to be far more formidable adversaries than bears.

Raccoons, which are clever and fastidious, can be both beguiling and infuriating in their antics. When you awake in the middle of the night to hear the sounds of little hands prying open your air-tight cookie canister or liberating the freshly-filleted walleye which you have carefully concealed in a covered fry pan—with a rock on top to prevent such things—more than likely it is the masked bandit at work. But these guys are not all work and no play, we decided.

We were camped on a small island in Algonquin Park in Ontario, islands often being recommended as campsites because of the very unlikelihood of nocturnal visitation. There is little that disturbs my slumber, but Dave, who is sensitive to every night sound, even a coming change in the weather, signaled by a shifting wind, seems to recall the suspicious sounds of midnight intruders. In view of our insular position, however, he chose to dismiss the telltale sounds and went back to sleep. The next morning we came out of our tents to find two loaves of bread done in, flour dusting the forest floor, the sugar sampled, and to add insult to injury, the pots and pans strewn far and wide. Reminiscent of Halloween mischief night, toilet paper festooned the campsite—the ultimate raccoon mockery.

OTHER ANIMALS

The beaver is a favorite of the kids. The evidence of his work is usually present everywhere; the distinctively gnawed tree stumps, the beaver dams which can change an entire landscape, and their architecturally impressive houses. Beavers are thought of as small animals, and it is a surprise to see them in the flesh. Some of the large males may weigh close to seventy pounds. The slap of their broad tails—a signal of warning—sounds like a twenty-pound boulder being dropped into the water.

Another appealing inhabitant of the north woods is the otter, who also leaves plenty of evidence with his slides— indeed, otter-slides! The first time you and the kids come upon this sleek fellow, his head bobbing up and down in the water, fifty yards from your canoe, you may be reminded of a small sea serpent. It is only when you realize that it is a friendly and curious otter that the initial shock subsides.

The moose personifies all that we associate with the northern wilderness. No kid, or adult for that matter, can fail to be impressed by the size, and almost prehistoric aura of these animals. Even with a noisy crowd in your canoe, you are likely to come across a browsing moose at a time when your crew is subdued—early in the morning or at dusk. A moose feeding in the shallow weedy bays or grazing at the river's edge just as you round the bend will provide your most likely encounter. Since they seem to enjoy eating more than they dislike interruption, they will often just keep on eating after your arrival. We sat with our kids in two canoes no more than twenty yards from one such gourmand as we cranked off a full reel of movie film. We think he left because we ran out of film.

Wildlife watching is really an acquired art. It is best to read enough to familiarize the group with the type of wildlife to expect and where to expect to see it. Work on training the eye to pick up movement rather than to look for shapes—then you too can learn the secrets of the forests.

8: First aid, safety, and conditioning

Forth then issued Hiawatha,
Wandered eastward, wandered westward,
Teaching men the use of simples
And the antidotes for poisons,
And the cure of all diseases.
Thus was first made known to mortals
All the mastery of Medamin,
All the sacred art of healing.

Hiawatha, or someone with his knowledge, would have been a valuable companion on one of our early trips. We had put the children to bed after dinner, read them their good night story, and were stealing a few moments together enjoying the final rays of the setting sun and the dying embers of the campfire. It was unusually quiet in the tent, and some premonition caused us to investigate. We discovered, to our horror, that our four-year-old had not been asleep at all, but had amused himself by emptying the contents of my pack. The first-aid kit was in disarray, a large bottle of children's aspirin, starkly empty (this was in the dark ages before child-proof tops).

What to do? We were a good day's paddle to the nearest road, and yet another three hours to the nearest town. My first-aid kit in those days was the commercial variety; lots of Band-Aids and ammonia inhalants, but nothing for a situation like this. In the recesses of my chaotic mind, I recalled my mother feeding me an evil concoction of baking soda and lemon juice to induce vomiting. Improvising we substituted baking powder and Tang, mixed with lake water and forcibly persuaded our son to ingest the vile stuff.

It did its work, and although he slept well that night, I spent a sleepless night watching him. He was fine, but I learned a good lesson. Shortly after returning home, I enrolled in a first-aid course. The lesson learned is this: had we been thinking prevention, it never would have happened. On the trail, as at home, aspirin and medications should never be left where small, exploring fingers can find them. First-aid training would have taught me ways to induce vomiting, including simple-to-use Syrup of Ipecac. Had there been a dose of this in our kit, there would have been no panic; just administer the Ipecac and await the results.

BEING PREPARED

On a canoe trip a town or hospital is not always around the corner. One may well have to rely on oneself for the small emergencies. The American Red Cross offers courses in first aid, from a short, basic course to the most advanced emergency care. One parent would do well to take at least a basic Red Cross course. In spite of a strategy of prevention, accidents still happen. Someone in your group should be in a position to make an educated assessment of the emergency, and have the knowledge to implement appropriate first aid. You also need a supply of the necessary materials, packed in an appropriate container and stored in an accessible place.

In preparing for a canoe trip of several days' duration, or more, it would be sensible for members of your party to have a physical checkup, and to tend to such matters as a current tetanus immunization, a bothersome back, or other chronic discomfort, muscular, respiratory or dental. While visiting your family doctor you have a great opportunity to get some expert advice: have him go over your list of first-aid supplies, for example. He may have suggestions for re-placing an item or two, with something newer or less ex-pensive, or be able to recommend the specific medication for one of your family members. An example might be an antihistamine for a child known to be especially sensitive to bites or stings.

In compiling our list of first-aid supplies (at the end of this chapter), we made an effort to find medications in the dry form to avoid spillage, and to select drugs with the broadest possible coverage and least possible side effects. Prescription drugs must be used with great care, as many of the drugs listed, when taken together, can have an adverse effect on the recipient. A combination can magnify the desired action, resulting in dangerous side effects. Avoid giving or taking more than one drug at a time. Twenty minutes to a half-hour should be allowed for the drug to take effect. The drugs on my list are obtainable only by a doctor's prescription, and your interview with your doctor is also the time to discuss with him the different drugs, their effects and side effects, and possible dangerous com-binations.

Bear in mind that I have included everything that might conceivably be needed for a month-long voyage in the remotest corner of the continent. Few trips, no matter how remote, will find you more than twelve hours from help; therefore, it would be inappropriate to take most of the prescriptions listed, and there is even less likelihood of your needing any of the injectables.

PACKING THE FIRST-AID KIT

How do you pack this weird assortment of bottles, boxes and soft goods? Through the years, we have experimented with tackle boxes, waterproof bags, and waterproof boxes. A small tackle box seems to be the most convenient for holding the medications. Each little bottle or other con-tainer, along with nail clippers and Q-Tips, fits securely into its own compartment. Beneath, there is room for your

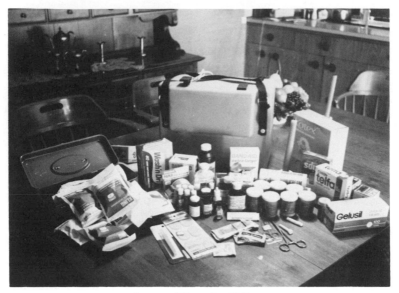

An expedition-sized kit.

thermometer, pocket flashlight, scissors, Ace bandage, or jar of Vaseline.

I label everything in the first-aid kit, not just with contents, but with directions for use, and notations on possible reactions and side effects. All the bulk dressings are packed in Ziploc bags and grouped together according to possible need; for example, Band-Aids, gauze pads, butterflies, and adhesive tape for cuts or lacerations. For a short trip, the tackle box should hold everything; otherwise, the tackle box may be one component in a larger waterproof bag. The kit should be enclosed in something waterproof in any case, and it should be put where you can get at it fast; not after twenty minutes of digging in the bottom of the food pack. Your kit can be a sizable investment, so think about leaving it packed to be used both for canoe outings and as a kit to be left in the car in case of accident. We replace all used items on our return home and update all the medications each year.

Canoe tripping with kids

CANOE TRIP HAZARDS

Thousands of people take canoe trips with no knowledge of first aid and carrying only the barest of first-aid equipment, and the likelihood of a serious mishap is slight. But the family that intends to take many, or increasingly difficult trips will rest a good deal easier if they are prepared for any eventuality.

In years of canoeing with kids we have learned to cope with a wide range of mishaps, including allergic reactions to bug bites, fishhooks in the finger, minor burns, and the usual gamut of cuts, scratches and bruises. On one trip we had to remove sutures from a pre-trip accident, since not all accidents happen in the woods. In fact, you are likely to be taking your greatest risk driving to the put-in.

There are probably no more hazards along a canoe route than within a four-block radius of your home, but we have found ourselves trying to minimize the chances of accidents by constantly reminding the kids not to run in the woods, for example. Walk the portage. Never step on something that can be stepped over.

Hypothermia

Our most serious crisis occurred on a trip without the kids, but it is worth repeating. On an extremely remote wilderness river, two of our companions lost a canoe in the rapids. The water temperature was in the mid-forties. The couple were suddenly stranded in chest-deep water attempting to free the canoe and rescue the packs. After getting them to shore we recognized the signs of hypothermia, and had to treat them.

What is hypothermia? We hear a lot about it but not many know what it is. It is the severe lowering of the body temperature, due to heat-loss that exceeds the body's ability to produce heat. Our bodies are very efficient heat machines, normally. Muscular activity increases heat output, and food increases the body's ability to generate heat (this provides paddlers with a great excuse to nibble from the gorp bag along their way on a cold, windy day).

As the body cools below normal body temperature of 98.6 degrees Fahrenheit (37° Celsius) the internal thermostat tells the body to shunt the blood from the extremities; it gets too cold, too fast, out there, resulting in a cooling of the core. Then, you shiver to generate more heat, but shivering wastes a lot of fuel and is a very inefficient means of making heat. Next, your arms and legs become tired and heavy due to a lack of oxygen being transported to chilled extremities, so the body tries harder; violent shivering, with impaired mental and physical functioning, are accompanied by apathy, listlessness, and sleepiness. Unconsciousness may follow, and should the core temperature go below 85 degrees F., death may occur.

What causes hypothermia? Generally, it takes a combination of three factors: cold, wet, and wind. The cold need not be extreme, when in combination with the others. Cold water next to the skin absorbs body heat thirty-two times faster than air of the same temperature. That is why we encourage the layered system for clothing and warmth, remembering that wool is the best for maintaining body heat when wet.

Still air is a very poor thermal conductor, so standing or sitting in a windless area, one can tolerate very low temperatures for some time. Wind is another matter, and, in combination with cold can become a problem. If the chilling effect of 20 degrees F. is combined with a wind of 35 miles per hour, it is equal to the chilling effect of −20 degrees F. with no wind. This effect is called the wind-chill factor. This factor should be taken into consideration on those early spring and late fall trips, when the temperature drops and the wind and rain pick up. This is not the time to make an extra ten miles. Consider your young crew members and stop early. Have lots of snacks handy, and encourage them to stay active. Being aware of the dangers of hypothermia will help you to be prepared, which includes staying dry, dressing appropriately, and knowing

Canoe tripping with kids

how to recognize its signs and effect treatment.

What if the worst should happen and one of the kids should slide into the chilly water in quest of a giant tadpole, and spend several minutes thrashing about? Strip and towel-dry the frozen Neptune, and place him in a pre-warmed sleeping bag. Someone can do this while the victim is stripped and dried. Hot liquid should be prepared and fed to him if he is conscious; but absolutely no alcohol. If the body temperature doesn't begin to climb within five minutes, the addition of another person to the bag is necessary, since the body has lost its ability to generate its own heat.

Kids lose body heat at a much greater rate than adults, and survival will depend on many variables: water temperature; amount of time in the water (in our example above, Junior was probably not in great danger, unless he was in for five minutes or more with a water temperature of sixty degrees, or less); body size; fat content; level of activity in the water. Thrashing around, or even swimming, drains body reserves very quickly. Fat people cool slower than thin people; big people, slower than little people. The key to re-warming is to heat from the inside out. Get the victim into a warm place, into a sleeping bag, and feed him some hot liquids. Hot-water bottles or warm blankets next to the trunk will help. Don't rub extremities in an attempt to generate heat, and don't forget to pre warm the sleeping bag. Check body temperature periodically to see if the victim is warming.

ANTICIPATE THE HAZARDS

There are many excellent books on wilderness emergencies, and several are listed in our bibliography. Outlining every conceivable disaster, however, will not prevent some new combination of unforeseen events from happening. Therefore, the best protection you can take to the woods with you is a basic knowledge of first-aid procedures, a cool head, and a workable first-aid kit. In safety—as in first aid—an ounce of prevention is worth a pound of cure, so we should review some of the personal skills you will need, and some of the hazards of which you should be aware.

For starters, can everyone in the family swim? Are they Red Cross "water safe," and do they know the HELP (heat-escape lessening posture), a fetal position maintained while floating in cold water? Even the youngest member of the family can learn basic water skills. In many towns, the Y offers a "waterbaby class." Does each member of the crew have a Type III PFD, and does everybody wear PFDs when they are on the water? For the very young, with a propensity for falling in, this means wearing the PFD all the time, treated like another layer of clothing.

Paddlers should be in control of their canoes at all times. This means being able to reach shore when a storm suddenly comes up while lake paddling. Can you make shore before the storm reaches you? What about rapids? If you enter them, you should be prepared to run them, but have you scouted them, and are you reasonably sure you can navigate them? If you do enter the rapids, can you and all in your boat swim the entire rapid in case of an upset?

High Water, Cold, Obstacles, and Reversals

Are you aware of the four main river hazards? *High water* is a product of springtime. Cold, swollen rivers are a danger, no matter how pleasant the day. It is not the best environment for novices. The same placid stream you paddled in the fall can become a torrent in the spring. Know your river and the possibilities of a sudden rise in water level from a melting snow pack, a dam release, or a good, hard rain. *Cold,* as we mentioned earlier, can cause hypothermia, and cold water needs to be treated with respect. What about *strainers* and *sweepers?* These are brush, fallen trees, bridge pilings or anything that allows the water current to flow through, but that could pin the

Canoe tripping with kids

boat or boater. The water pressure on anything trapped in this manner makes rescue difficult, if not impossible. Last, but not least, are *weirs* (low dams), *reversals* and *souse holes,* which occur when water rushes over an obstacle and then curls back on itself in a stationary wave, as when water flows over a dam. The surface water below the dam is actually flowing back upstream, and its action can trap anything floating between the drop and the wave. Once trapped in this manner, a swimmer's only chance may be to dive below the surface of the water where the current is flowing downstream, or try and swim out at the end of the wave.

This is not meant to paralyze prospective canoe trippers with fear, but to strongly suggest the importance of recognizing that dangers do exist and that, in addition to common sense and canoeing skills appropriate to the difficulty of the proposed trip, you should have obtained first-hand information about your intended route which is both accurate and up-to-date. Other competent canoers, rather than the local night crawler merchant, are the best source of information about such hazards as high water, rapids, dams, or a recently downed tree, as well as the location of the portages and advance landmarks. Almost any river trip should be preceded by a checking with knowledgeable, first-hand sources.

PHYSICAL CONDITIONING

What about physical conditioning for a canoe trip? A conditioning program should be entirely personal, depending on the type of trip contemplated, the level of fitness you maintain, the ages of the kids, and their normal activity level. As in any sport, adequate physical preparation will ensure your enjoyment and will reduce the likelihood of injuries. It would be miserable for Dad to pull a back muscle the first day out, trying to lift a seventy-pound canoe onto his shoulders for a portage.

On the other hand, canoeing and canoe tripping is not

an ordeal, and can be designed not to be one. There are many of us who have taken trips over the years, who have gotten in shape as we went along. We planned our early days to be short and without portages. We sprinkled in enough rest days, and allowed enough leeway in our miles-per-day planning to counteract possible sore muscles. With each succeeding day, our muscles toned, and our ability to relax and rebuild our strength for the next day increased. Our food packs also diminished in size and weight. By the trip's end we could manage longer days and longer portages. Here again, common sense is your best guide.

LIST OF FIRST-AID SUPPLIES

Prescription Drugs and Special Items for Extended Wilderness Trips (Must be prescribed by a physician)

Demerol (injectable) for pain

Novocain (injectable) for local pain

disposable syringes

Donnatal—for severe indigestion

codeine—for pain

Thorazine (suppositories and tablets) for nausea and vomiting

paregoric—for diarrhea

Gantrisin—for urinary infection

Pyridium—for bladder infection

Erythromycin—for infection

Modane—for constipation

threaded curved suture needles (3-0 and 5-0), mosquito clamps and scalpels

Standard Items for the First-Aid Kit

Chlortrimeton—an antihistamine for bug bites and allergic reactions

Burows Solution—for ear infections

Alcaine—anaesthetic for eye injury

an antibiotic for eye infection

Syrup of Ipecac—to induce vomiting

aspirin

Oil of Clove and Cavitt—for lost fillin
   (ask your dentist)
Rhuli Cream—topical to relieve itching
nasal spray
Merthiolate—for cuts and scratches
peroxide
Vaseline
zinc oxide, chap stick and sunscreen—to
antacid—for stomach upset
small scissors and small flashlight
thermometer
elastic bandages—both 2-inch and 4-inch sizes
gauze pads—2- by 2-inch, 4- by 4-inch, and several large
   combo dressings
roller gauze, 1- and 2-inch
Band-Aids and butterflies
snakebite kit—where approprite

Pack in an appropriate container and store in an accessible place.

BIBLIOGRAPHY FOR FIRST AID AND SAFETY

WILKERSON, JAMES. *Medicine for Mountaineering,* The Mountaineers, Seattle, Washington, 1967.

KODET, E. RUSSELL, and BRADFORD ANGIER. *Being Your Own Wilderness Doctor,* Stackpole Books, Harrisburg, Pennsylvania, 1968.

KEATING, W. R. *Survival in Cold Water: The Physiology and Treatment of Immersion Hypothermia and of Drowning,* Blackwell Scientific Publication, Oxford, England, 1969.

GRAVES, RICHARD H. *Bushcraft: A Serious Guide to Survival and Camping,* Schocken Books, New York, 1972.

American Red Cross, *Advanced First Aid and Emergency Care,* Doubleday and Company, New York, 1973.

Emergency Care and Transportation of the Sick and Injured, by the American Academy of Orthopaedic Surgeons, 1971.

9: Canoe skills for family tripping

Paddles none had Hiawatha,
Paddles none he had or needed,
For his thoughts as paddles served him;
And his wishes served to guide him;
Swift or slow at will he glided,
Veered to right or left at pleasure.

We can't state precisely at what age the kids graduate from baggage to paddlers; maybe when you are no longer able to stuff them amongst the packs, or when the freeboard on your canoe has reached a dangerous minimum, described momentarily. For almost four years, and we started our kids right out of diapers, four of us fit somewhat snugly in a 15-foot, wood and canvas Chestnut canoe that was 37 inches at the beam and weighed a mere 55 pounds.

HOW MANY CANOES?

The major determinant of when you move to two canoes is ease of portaging and who is available to portage. If that task is going to fall to you alone, and if a contemplated trip is going to involve a number of long portages—and I would consider anything over five hundred yards or a quarter-mile, long—you will think twice about expanding the fleet beyond one boat. There are well-designed seventeen-foot canoes available on the market today which will comfortably accommodate two adults, two little persons, and all the food and gear for a week's outing. Comfort will depend on the weight of the adults and the extent to which they try to pack along an entire suburban support system.

The interim step to expanding the fleet and the captains and first mates is to have your junior passengers take up paddling from their positions amidships. This can be somewhat confusing if there is more than one, but here you must use your ingenuity, and patience. You will be amazed at the additional motive power that one diminutive paddler can provide. Even if your junior can only contribute a total of one hour during a paddling day, you're that much further ahead.

A TRIM CANOE

You will arrange paddlers, passengers, and duffel in the canoe with several objectives in mind, and with some obvious constraints. The major objectives are comfort and safety. The essence of safety is a low center of gravity and

A good recreational canoe design will comfortably accommodate two adults and two young kids.

adequate freeboard (see below). If you are going to have a kid paddling from amidships, he or she is going to have to be a reasonable distance off the floor of the canoe, and offset toward the gunwale of the canoe so that the kid's paddle can reach the water without requiring unnatural contortions and without stubbing knuckles on the gunwales. This means positioning packs to provide a seat, and distributing the weight to offset the off-center seating of your third paddler/passenger.

To the extent that you can lay the other packs flat in the bottom of the boat—the less showing above the top of the gunwale line the better—you will compensate for the instability of having three bodies flailing away from their erect positions. If your kids are still in the advanced creeper stage, it is best to keep them as near to the bottom of the canoe as possible. You might provide them with miniature paddles, as a ceremonial gesture. In our experience these get precious little use but give the kids a sense of self-importance and belonging.

Good life preservers are not only a must, but provide a cushion for the kids' backs if they are up against the center thwart. Whether your center person is in front of or behind the center thwart will depend on the design of the canoe and the placement of the thwarts. In packing the canoe you will be concerned with the trim (a level canoe when viewed from either end) as well as the attitude of bow and stern. If the man is going to be in the stern, and outweighs his bow partner by forty pounds, the canoe gear, as well as the passengers, need to be distributed so as to

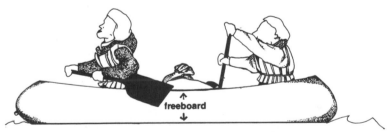

A trim canoe rides level in the water and has at least 6 inches of freeboard (clear space between the water line and the gunwale at the midpoint of the canoe) when fully loaded.

result in a canoe whose bow and stern are level with each other.

"Freeboard" was mentioned, and having plenty of it is not only good safety sense, but means less effort needed to move and to maneuver the canoe through the water. Viewed from the side, there should be a minimum of six inches of freeboard, or clear space between the water line and gunwale at the midpoint of the canoe.

The comfort of your little passengers is important. You will be off to a great start if all of your ingenuity is applied to keeping them warm and dry. At a minimum activity level, they will have to be dressed more warmly than their paddling counterparts, and it is important to have them on some sort of pad or a flat pack, so that their behinds are not like a wick dipped into the inevitable puddle in the bottom of the canoe. Aluminum canoes, in particular, act as an efficient conductor of chilly water temperatures, and a bottom-pad is especially important for passengers in them. A poncho that covers your passenger entirely will permit him or her to contract into a fetal position within its folds and will be invaluable protection from all but the foulest weather, in which case, you ought to be off the water anyway.

The success of your packing and positioning of packs and passenger(s) will be measured by how much shut-eye is logged by your kids. The gentle slap of wavelets on the bottom of your canoe is an almost infallible opiate to usually restless kids. We have paddled for hours with our kids sound asleep on the floor of the canoe, only to awaken when the canoe was dragged ashore at lunch time or at the end of the day.

PLANNING AROUND THE MILEAGE AND PORTAGES

The actual skills needed on the water are perhaps less important than planning a trip around your personnel and abilities of the players. For those first trips, your objective will be quiet waters, protected ponds and lakes, and meandering streams. You will want to carefully calculate the mileage, size and configuration of the lakes, and the number and length of the portages.

If you are traveling with little ones whose only baggage will be small personal packs—meaning that you and your wife are the chief packers and porters—and if you expect several portages, you should plan on no more than five to ten miles per day; perhaps a fifty-mile trip in a week's time. As the motive power and carrying capacity of your family increases, you can expect to increase your mileage to ten to fifteen miles a day. As experience builds, longer portages and larger lakes can be considered; river trips, and, later, rapids are possible.

Age and experience will have a bearing on your mileage expectations, but the size of your crew will, too. The rule is: the larger the group, the slower it moves. The corollary is that the tendency to putter is the square of the number by which the crew exceeds four. There will be lost tennis shoes, air mats that will not deflate, breakfast scraps for the camp jays, and the sudden urge to stalk the lunker pike. On the day for which you have planned to cover fifteen rigorous miles, the cry for pancakes will arise in unison; a breakfast that requires every pot in the kit and half a morning to prepare.

Even with an optimum crew size, part of canoe trip planning is to assume that obstacles and diversions will invariably arise to thwart your best-laid plans. A rainstorm will pin you down, a portage trail will elude your search, or good fishing will arrest your progress. Therefore, plan for the delays, and plan for breaks or rest days to enjoy a midcourse discovery such as a fishing hole or an inviting campsite.

More than any other single factor, the number and length of portages will affect your planning. We will get into some of the finer points of mastering the portage in the next chapter, but a few additional comments on preparation are in order. The efficiency with which you move will be a direct result of your success in organizing and consolidating packs to end up with the fewest number, consistent with the load-carrying capabilities of each of your crew. Do a little simple arithmetic. Add up the number of canoes and packs (or loads, since it is often possible to carry more than one pack at a time), and divide by the number of able-bodied canoers. If your answer is greater than two, plan again! If the portages are all short—five hundred yards, or less—tripling (making three trips across) the portages is not completely out of the question. It may just be unavoidable.

There is little you can do to rearrange the geography of your canoeing destination, but it is often possible to plan the route so that the longer portages are at the end of the trip. By that time you and your paddlers will have toughened up, and weighty food packs will have been considerably reduced in size.

If you and your family have attained the necessary skills to tackle larger lakes and moving water, twenty or more miles a day is reasonable. River currents of three to five miles per hour can give your fleet quite a push, providing there are no major obstacles, such as dams and waterfalls, or rapids requiring scouting; all three of which may call for a portage. It may then be that location and frequency of campsites are the limiting factors.

CANOEING SKILLS FOR PROTECTED (QUIET) WATERS

There are many varied canoe trips that can be undertaken by a family group possessing only moderate or basic canoeing skills. The observance of safe canoeing practices, including good equipment and the wearing of life preservers are at least as important as having a good "J" stroke, in fact, more so. Let's cover some of those basics, and get ready for our first outing.

Entrances and Exits

Earlier we covered the principles of loading and positioning gear and passengers; all designed to preserve as low a center of gravity as possible, and to achieve a trim hull. Whether you are loading people or baggage, the canoe should be afloat. Loading a canoe high and dry on shore, and dragging it across the rocks for the launch is tough on the canoe and poor canoemanship.

Only one person should enter or exit a canoe at a time, and a thoughtful partner will hold the canoe while his or her companion climbs in or out, or loads the packs. Climbing into the canoe, the paddler should grab the gunwales and lower himself into the seat. If you enter the canoe fore or aft of the seat keep your hands on both gunwales and advance them toward the seat, a method that may prevent unseemly acrobatics. More damaged canoes, and more wet canoers, occur at the put-ins and landing spots than in all the rapids and rainstorms in canoedom. Sometimes, a safe and efficient loading or landing will require that one or more of you get your feet wet, which is usually preferable to a damaged canoe, or watching your bow paddler or child go sailing into the drink.

A thoughtful partner will hold the canoe while his or her partner climbs in or out.

The Basic Paddle Strokes

Six basic strokes: three for the stern and three for the bow, will provide ample tools for canoeing quiet waters. The stern strokes are the *straight*, or *power* stroke, the *stern pry*, and the *stern sweep*. A fourth stroke, the "J", is a useful technique, but not essential. Both the stern pry—when used as a ruddering device—and the "J" are meant to correct for the canoe's natural tendency to veer away from the stern paddler's paddling side. This tendency is a measure of the directional instability of most canoe designs (deep-V'd, long-keeled racing hulls being a notable exception), and, more importantly, to the fact of the stern paddler's greater leverage.

Good canoeing practice calls for bow and stern paddler to pick a side to paddle on, and stick with it. Each partner will choose his strong or natural side, if possible, but often one person will have to make an adjustment. The reason for not switching sides, except as an occasional ploy to rest fatigued muscles, is that the bow and stern paddlers will learn complementary strokes, ones which, when they are executed together, will cause the canoe to move most efficiently in the desired direction. Let's consider the basic strokes that drive the canoe in a straight line.

The Power Stroke. The straight-ahead, or power strokes for both the bow and stern paddler are essentially the same; however, the bow may use a faster cadence, ending the stroke at the hips. The stern paddler will leave his paddle in the water and finish off his stroke with a correcting pry or "J", to keep the canoe on a straight track. For short distances, almost any form of execution will suffice to move the canoe, but canoe trippers need to observe some simple techniques to minimize fatigue over the longer distances— you'll also want enough energy left over for making dinner, setting up camp, etc. The trick is to use your back in paddling, as well as your arms. Extending your body forward from the hips as you reach to plant your paddle, and bringing your upper body back in concert with the paddle blade, will put you into harmony with your canoe, give you greater control, and permit you to tick off many more effortless miles.

The Stern Pry. Every two or three strokes, the stern will need to correct for the veering tendency of the canoe. The simplest means is the *stern pry* (sometimes referred to as as a *push away*), which merely converts the tail end of the power stroke into a rudder. As the paddle comes past the stern paddler's hips, he places the fleshy base of the palm on the gunwale behind him and twists the paddle grip with his upper hand to turn the front, or non-power face of the paddle blade away from the side of the canoe. Using the point at which the lower hand is holding the paddle to the gunwale as the fulcrum, the paddler pulls the top of the paddle toward his chest, causing the non-power face of the blade to pry outward, moving the stern in the opposite direction. A variation can be performed without using the gunwale, the paddle merely being turned so that that the non-power face can be used to "push away" from the side of the canoe. This maneuver has the same effect as the pry, but lacks the leverage potential of the pry. Momentarily, we will see how the pry is used to make the boat turn sharply.

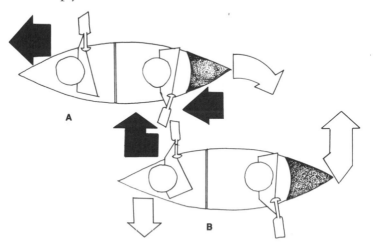

A. Canoe has tendency to "veer" away from stern paddler's side.
B. Stern pry corrects by pushing or ruddering the stern back into line.

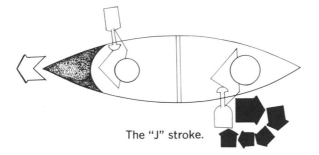

The "J" stroke.

The "J" Stroke. The pry is the simplest correcting stroke, and has other uses as well. In whitewater it becomes a staple. However, generations of canoers have learned to use the "J" as the basic cruising stroke. For me it is a change of pace, or resting stroke (sort of like using a side stroke in swimming) used on the few occasions when Judy and I switch sides.

It is not long before most people start to develop their own techniques and paddling modes to combat fatigue, or simply as an extension of their own physical idiosyncrasies, so any attempts to describe the "right way" to paddle would be doomed to failure. Here, nonetheless, is how I would describe the "J" stroke.

The "J" does it all with the back, or power face of the paddle, as opposed to the stern pry, which uses the non-power face of the paddle to move the stern over. The initiation of the "J" starts almost immediately after the commencement of the forward stroke, the paddle pushed downward, as well as pulled back. Before your paddle reaches the hips you will cock your lower wrist hard and turn your upper palm outward (away from the boat), causing the blade to "catch" at the bottom, or upturn, of the "J". You will be pulling your blade up and away from the canoe, with the blade coming out of the water already feathered, to return for the next stroke (the "feathered" blade is carried with its edge leading, forward on a non-wind-resistant plane with the water). Look at the diagram, and re-read the components of the stroke, but it's one you will have to learn by doing. In time it becomes so natural that an observer would be unaware of any special motion being used to keep the canoe in a straight line. In fact, to the extent that your correcting strokes, whether "J" or pry, are executed quickly and efficiently, you will eliminate the zigging and zagging that can add tiring miles to your canoeing day.

The Stern Sweep. If the stern pry and the "J" stroke were used to turn the canoe *toward* the paddle side, the *stern sweep* will accelerate the turn of the canoe *away* from the paddling side, that is, in the direction it would veer if only forward or uncorrected power strokes were used. The stern paddler, by extending the paddle as far out from the canoe as possible, and sweeping it in a broad arc, fore-to-aft, puts an even longer handle on the lever, increasing the turning impetus. Every now and then, this may be used as a "correcting" stroke to compensate for wind or a chance, overpowering stroke on the part of the bow paddler when the canoe needs to be turned away from the stern paddler's side. More often, however, it is a turning stroke, for which the bow paddler's complementary move is a *draw stroke.*

The Draw Stroke. Up to now our bow paddler has been providing non-complaining, forward motive power, as he stern-pried, swept, and "J"-stroked across the lake. However, the time has come to turn around and head back. The draw stroke, whether performed by the bow or stern, is a means of pulling your end of the canoe over. The bow paddler, in this case, will reach out over his gunwale, planting the paddle blade well away, and facing the hull, pulling himself and the canoe to the paddle. Be sure to get the paddle out of the water before it goes under the canoe, with you right behind. Draw strokes are more of a necessity on moving water, and particularly on tight streams or rivers, where their execution is quite vigorous, but for docking and positioning the canoe they are a canoer's bread and butter. Flat water is the place to learn these and every stroke.

110

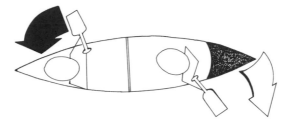

The stern sweep increases the stern paddler's leverage, causing the canoe to turn sharply away from his paddling side.

A

The drawstroke from the bow (a) moves the bow over (b), and when complemented by a draw in the stern, the canoe pivots sharply (c).

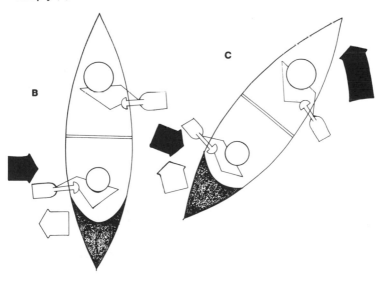

B

C

Take note that if the bow and the stern paddler execute the draw on their respective sides, the result will be a very smart turn.

SKILLS FOR MOVING WATER

Moving water includes lakes where the wind has raised a moderate chop, and streams or rivers with good current, but no rapids of consequence. Whitecapped lakes are definitely to be avoided and route planning should seek also to avoid committing your party to open reaches more than half a mile from a shoreline, in the case of a sudden squall or rising wind.

Running rapids can certainly be a part of family canoeing, but it requires water-reading and paddling skills of a high order. Until those skills are acquired, good judgment calls for walking around all rapids of Class II difficulty or greater. Class II water, according to the International Scale of River Difficulty, contains easy rapids with waves up to three feet, and wide clear channels that are obvious without scouting. Even the latter must be treated with the greatest respect, particularly for family groups, whose early excursions should be restricted to smaller lakes and rivers of no greater than Class I difficulty; Class I is described as "moving water with a few riffles and small waves. Few or no obstructions."

Let's take a look at wind and lakes. Even with the best planning, you must be prepared to deal with windy and ruffled waters. A tiny lake can be whipped up in no time by high, gusting winds that can arise without warning. They present no great danger, but can be frustrating to simple forward progress. An empty canoe, occupied by two paddlers of unequal weight, in which the weight distribution causes the bow to rise out of the water, is a natural windvane. Even moderate wind gusts will catch hold of the bow and tend to pivot the canoe on its stern to align the canoe with the direction of the wind (hence, the wind-

Canoe tripping with kids

Moderate rapids can be run with the kids, but to do so without the necessary skills and experience is foolhardy. Note the young bow paddler is about to do a cross draw—probably to move the bow to the left, in line with a new channel.

vane effect). If that is different from the paddlers' intended course, they've got frustration. The solution to this is a trim (described earlier in the chapter) or slightly bow-heavy canoe, and having the paddlers move down off their seats.

Quartering

If the wave tops are beginning to be flecked with white, or if forward progress is becoming difficult, it is time to get off the water and wait it out. Even a moderate headwind, however, requires an adjustment of technique, known as "quartering." This calls for canoers to paddle into the wind at a slight angle, rather than head on, which has the effect of flattening out the troughs and peaks of the waves and minimizes the rise and fall of the bow. Your bow partner will

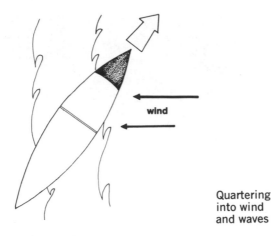

Quartering
into wind
and waves

appreciate not being dropped, every fourth wave, into a
waiting trough and getting a gallon of lake splashed into
the lap. Here too, a kneeling position, and packs and passengers organized for the lowest center of gravity, will enhance your comfort and ability to make headway.

Little Rivers

Small meandering streams, for a day trip or encountered on
a week's canoe trip, are a delight and a challenge. Every
bend brings a new view and the likelihood of surprising a
deer or moose browsing. Every bend also brings a new
test of paddling skills, but without severe penalties for ineptness; perhaps a hangup on the gravel bar at the inside
of the bend or momentary entanglement in the alder bushes
at the outside of the bend. (In heavier currents, and with
more unyielding obstructions, there can be more serious
consequences—Chapter 8, on safety.) On such streams, complementary pairs of bow and stern strokes, such as the draw
described earlier, or combination of stern pry and bow
cross draw (a new stroke), must be executed sharply and in
anticipation of sharp bends and hairpin turns.

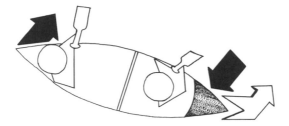

The stern pry (absent the forward or straight part of the stroke), executed in combination with a bow cross draw, turns the canoe sharply to the left or right when the strokes are executed on the other side of the canoe.

The stern pry was described earlier as a means of correcting, to achieve a straight line. In order to sharply turn the canoe, you must either execute several pries in quick succession—leaving out the straight portion of the stroke—or continue pushing away with the non-power face of your paddle, until the canoe has made its turn. The earlier admonishment was for paddlers to pick a side and stick with it; however, on tight little rivers it may be necessary for the stern paddler to switch to the opposite side to pry—complemented by the bow partner's draw stroke—since it is a more powerful turning stroke than the sweep.

The *cross draw*, used only by the bow paddler, is perhaps the most difficult of the basic strokes to master, but for tight maneuvering it is a must, and it is a far more effective tool than the cross-bow rudder (which is even more awkward!) taught by camps and instruction books for years. Without changing the paddle grip, the bow paddler simply puts the elbow of his upper arm into his ribs and sweeps the paddle blade over the bow. By twisting the upper body in the process, he punches out with the lower arm to plant the paddle blade three feet out from the side of the canoe and in a position to pull the boat toward the paddle. Both the draw and the cross draw will be more effective if the

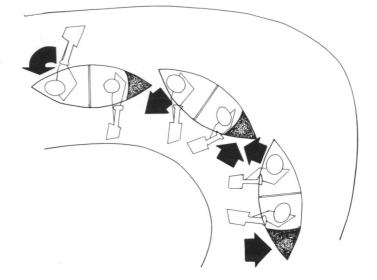

The stern starts to sweep and realizes that a more powerful stroke will be necessary to make the turn; switches sides and pries hard on his right gunwale. All the time, his bow partner is drawing to move the bow around.

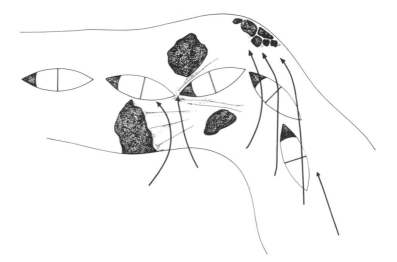

Setting around the bend to avoid being swept into the outside of the bend, and oriented to pass between the two waiting boulders.

paddler puts his body into the stroke, extending himself well out over the water. They who hesitate, or are tentative in their execution, are candidates for the alders or the sand bar—all of which is, of course, part of the learning process. And after you think you have mastered it all, some humbling encounters await you.

Bigger Rivers

On wide and sluggish rivers you will need no more canoe-handling skills than were required for little lakes, but when the gradient and volume of water flow increases to four, six or as much as eight miles per hour, even in the absence of rapids, you will want some additional skills in your paddling arsenal. Your first concern will be with safety precautions, the dangers associated with such obstructions as low dams, "sweepers" or downed trees, and the problems created by high water or low water temperatures.

If you have mastered the pry, the sweep and draw stroke described earlier, you are only partially armed to tackle a swiftly-moving river. Now you must be able to read the current and understand how the positioning of your canoe in relation to the current can be coordinated to get you down river, around bends and obstructions, and in overall control of your destiny and destination. Over time, you will learn to recognize the rhythm of a river as it oscillates from side to side, creating and guided by its channel. Take note of how it flows more swiftly at the outside of the bend, and slowly at the inside. Learn to recognize the "vee," or tongue pointing downstream to show you the way between two partially submerged boulders. Your objective will be to stay in the main current, away from shallow bars, while avoiding being swept into the outside of the bend, or into obstructions in the main channel.

Rounding a Bend. The positioning of a canoe for *setting around a bend* may call for some back paddling on the part of the canoers to keep the canoe in position, while the current does most of the work of moving the canoe. Every river and every bend is different, and the speed and volume of flow make for infinite combinations. With experience, you will begin to approach full mastery, but a recognition of the principles is the first step.

Crossing Rivers by Canoe. Easy to learn, and invaluable for large rivers with a good current, is the *upstream ferry*. It can be practiced, and its principles learned, in very moderate currents, and applied on increasingly swifter rivers as a means of attaining a downstream objective or crossing a river to a point directly opposite.

Paddlers should be able to "ferry" across a river without great exertion; primary attention being given to the angle of the canoe to the current. There is a point of equilibrium, where the combination of angle, canoe momentum (minimal), and downriver force of the current cause the canoe to move laterally across the river (the canoe in the diagram is angled to move from point A to B). On the Yukon where we were being swept along, sometimes in excess of eight miles per hour, our frequent objective was to hit a point on the river bank—perhaps our lunch stop—without getting carried downriver and out of reach of our objective. This meant bringing the canoe about, to face upstream (see the diagram), and then to "crab" or ferry our way to shore (at point C). The exact angle will be a matter of feel,

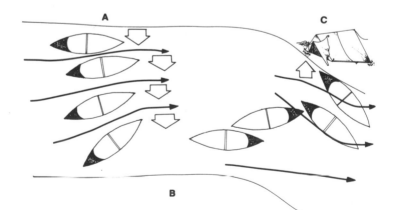

but generally, the swifter the current, the more acute the angle with the current required to effect the lateral movement of the canoe. An experienced team, adjusting their angle with the ever-changing strength of the current, can cross a tremendously strong rapid with amazing lateral speed, their angle so acute as to be imperceptible. A miscalculation and they are sent scurrying back the way they came, or turned broadside, and into trouble. Your family group will want to avoid waters of that vigor.

OTHER SKILLS

These come under two general categories: learning to recognize trouble [covered in more detail in Chapter 8] and the willingness to get wet. Trouble may be in the form of a thunderstorm or rising winds, or an otherwise docile river made treacherous by recent heavy rains. A nose for changes in the weather—to say nothing of an ability to recognize weather signs—is helpful. Eyes and ears on alert for the sound of falls, rapids or other obstructions, which even the best maps or knowledgeable first-hand reports inexplicably fail to mention, will be valuable allies.

Getting wet is another matter. No book on canoe tripping fails to describe the theory and practice of lining a canoe, using lines attached to bow and stern to let a canoe down through drops deemed to be unrunnable. Years of experience have taught us that if a drop can be lined cleanly—that is, without the liners' getting wet—it probably can be run. Otherwise you start out, per the instructions, with a person on bow and stern lines, and by restraining the bow or stern as the current catches the hull, the boat can actually be moved toward and away from the shore to dodge obstructions, all in the name of avoiding the agonies of unloading the canoes and portaging.

Often lining turns out to be a case of jumping knee deep into the water, Mom and Dad, brother and sister, each hanging on to a gunwale, and half dragging, half pushing and hauling the loaded canoe down a shallow,

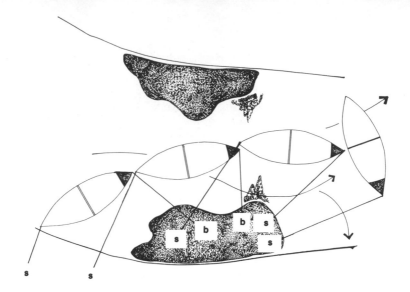

Letting down over a ledge and around a boulder, as bow and stern man control lines to adjust for downstream current, and orienting canoe to pass through the two obstructions. In the final sequence, the stern man lets go his line to allow the canoe to swing completely around on the bow man's tether. To hang on to the stern line risks putting the broadside of the canoe into conflict with the downstream current, and a sure capsize.

slippery set of ledges. Late in the summer, in the upper reaches of streams that ran crisp and gurgling, fully capable of carrying a loaded canoe earlier in the year, canoes are confronted with scratchy trickles, where only the willingness to get wet permits progress.

LEARNING

Canoeing is something that has to be learned by doing, and oftentimes the group approach is best. Taking part in classes offered by canoe dealers, college or club groups, or through camps and outdoor education programs, can benefit everybody. Such programs are more widely available than ever before, and we recommend them enthusiastically. Progressive learning is the key, whether learned on one's own and on the job, or formally, with a club or group. You will take on increasingly difficult waters as skills and experience are gradually enhanced.

Almost every major city, and some not so major, boasts a canoe club—usually an affiliate of the American Canoe Association (ACA). By joining a canoe club, you will have access to the club's trip schedule, which will indicate the degree of difficulty of each trip. You will be well advised to start on those novice trips where you are not likely to be a hazard to yourself or to your companions, and where there will be leisure and time to ask questions. Other canoers will be delighted to show you the strokes and give you advice on reading water. Many trips, in fact, are designated training trips.

If one is going to learn and practice the paddle strokes described in this chapter, it should be done on warm, quiet and shallow waters, and with an empty canoe. It should not be attempted under the duress of a cruising or tripping situation where the consequences of ineptness could result in unpleasant memories or inconvenience to

The stern paddler braces to slow and steady the canoe in whitewater. Here, mother and daughter negotiate a rapid on the Noatak River, Alaska.

more proficient canoeing companions. It would also be well to practice the strokes from the kneeling position, as this will provide you with both improved leverage and increased confidence. The lower center of gravity and body contact with the canoe will permit you to reach and execute vigorously, without danger of upset. As you master the principles and get the feel, you can move back to the seat.

A problem. Like most couples we started our canoeing careers in the typical male chauvinist tradition; husband in the stern—he's the captain, of course—and wife in the bow, presumably to provide uncomplaining, unquestioning horsepower. In this mode, deficiencies in technique could be overcome by loud and authoritative directives bellowed from the stern seat.

Well, here's the case for canoe instruction. Each person—husband, wife, brother, sister—needs to learn both the bow and stern strokes. At some point, some other member of your family is going to have to take the stern of one canoe, with a son or daughter as bow partner.

Depending on their ages, the kids can learn likewise, as your bow or stern partner, or on their own. If they are going to start out as baggage, teach them to sit quietly in the bottom of the canoe! If teaching your own kids is a frustrating exercise, as it is in many families, it is just as well to let them try it on their own, in pairs or solo. Just be sure the conditions are controlled, that they are wearing life preservers and are in warm, shallow, protected waters.

Short of standing up on the seats, or other purposeful attempts to overturn the canoe, the light weight of kids in relation to the buoyancy and stability of most recreational canoes is less likely to capsize your craft than is a sudden gust of wind. In fact, some purposeful upsets and playing with a swamped canoe are a good learning experience for the kids, to get all of you used to the idea that a swamped canoe is no big deal and that it is still a buoyant conveyance. A wind which suddenly transports your little ones halfway across the lake, may, on the other

The teenagers catch on fast.

The day arrives when the teenagers can take charge of their own canoe. Here, they find the "vee" between the ledge on their right and a boiling hole on their left.

hand, give everyone a scare. If this is even a remote possibility, the kids should be old enough and capable enough to understand the appropriate tactics described earlier; getting down on their knees, bow in the water (so as not to windvane), and knowing how to use a stern rudder or pry.

The fact is that the kids learn to control the canoe with amazing swiftness, even in the absence of hard instruction. This is attributable to the natural and logical reaction of canoe, paddler and paddle. As soon as they grasp a few simple principles and try it out for themselves, the learning curve is sharply upward. Your challenge will be to control the environment and provide progressively more demanding opportunities, without over-extending the limits of confidence and competence—yours or theirs.

With these basics in grasp, and mentally and physically equipped to take a canoe trip, let's get under way.

10: Underway

On the clear and luminous water
Launched his birch canoe for sailing,
From the pebbles of the margin
Shoved it forth into the water;
Whispered to it, "Westward! westward!"
And with speed it darted forward.

The planning is complete. You and your family have chosen for your canoe trip one of Canada's provincial parks for the last week of August and the first week of September. The waters will be warm and the mosquitoes and blackflies should be on the wane. Both your driving and canoeing route are cleverly designed around the expectation that the roads and parks will be crowded with people cramming in their last vacation days before school starts. Rather than planning a circle route which brings you back to the close-in lakes, where the weekend trippers are fighting over every available tent site, you have arranged with the outfitter to pick you up with his truck where an old logging road crosses Bog Creek, near the boundary of the park, which is otherwise closed to motor vehicle use.

This route permits you to penetrate further into the park's interior, where you can expect good fishing and fewer people. To make the final day's rendezvous with the outfitter's truck, you will have to portage three hundred yards in to a small pond and cross to the opposite side, where a short paddle upstream on a weedy creek will bring you to the elderly log bridge.

Your planning has been so meticulous and your execution so flawless that you now have several hours before the arrival of the truck to rearrange the packs, wash out the canoes, enjoy a light lunch with the last of the peanut butter, and best of all, to change into the last clean dry clothing, squirreled in the bottom of your pack for the occasion. The kids don fresh but wrinkled shirts, and your wife ties up her hair in a bright bandana.

After twelve days in the wilderness, the soreness of unused muscles during the first three days has given way to a firmer tone and sense of physical well-being. The confusion and awkwardness that marked the first days on the water have evolved into a family routine and division of labor, as your team has become more effective and confident, day by day. Heated debates among family members about when to stop for the day, where to camp, or the advisability of crossing a lake at its widest point, are forgotten as you look back on a successfully completed trip. One of the girls' air mattresses sprang a leak, and next year you vow to switch to foam, or at least carry a repair kit, but, somehow, this annoyance has been survived. When you discovered that both you and your son favored paddling on the right, one of you had to make the adjustment.

You were lucky the afternoon a sudden gust of wind picked up your beached canoe and sent it skittering down the lake shore. It was a warm sunny day and you were able to recover it quickly. From that point on you made sure that the canoes were pulled well up on shore *and* tied to a tree, whether stopped for lunch, or camped for the night.

The rumble of the truck, its dust rising above the trees, jars you from your reveries. It is a welcome sound, but there is also a wistful feeling that the adventure is at an end, and that the recent interlude during which your way of life was altered is only a memory. Now you must return to another reality, but you will do so with renewed vigor and an improved perspective. The paper clip wars being waged in corporate jungles are frivolous

Canoe tripping with kids

when compared to the essential and absorbing occupation of coaxing a fire from wet wood on a blustery evening, or struggling alongside your daughter to erect the tent in a summer thunderstorm.

ROUTE-FINDING

Armed with good maps, a trip description, and local advice from fishermen or outfitters, you should meet few navigation problems that the normally observant cannot take in stride. Usually, the outfitter can trace a route on the map, marking the portages, direction of river flow, likely campsites—including alternates if mileage should fall short of the plan. He can also point out any major changes in waterways or portage trails caused by washouts, unusually dry or wet weather, or even the rearrangement of an entire stream and pond system by industrious beavers.

River-running, of course, requires no route-finding in the sense of finding one's way. One will need information, however, as to velocity, water levels for the particular time of year, the nature and location of obstructions both natural and artificial, and, if there are rapids, falls or dams to be encountered, the location of the portage trail around them. "No Indian ever drowned on a portage" goes the adage, and when rapids are ahead, there should be no confusion as to when and where to get off the river. The canoers should know how far above the obstruction to be looking for the marks indicating the beginning of the portage, which often will take off well above the actual falls or rapid, cutting off an elbow in the river. On well-traveled rivers the portages are likely to be obvious and well marked, but as one reaches further into the back country, the signs become less obvious, and the penalties for error more severe.

Your early trips should be particularly selective when rivers are contemplated, but one should not be scared off by rivers. There are countless miles of quiet, meandering streams where only the direction of growth of the weeds on the bottom betrays the current's direction, and it is on the rivers and streams, as each bend and elbow brings a new view, that paddlers are likely to see an abundance of bird life and water fowl; to see fish darting under the canoe; or to surprise a moose feeding in the shallows.

River Reading

Often rapids turn out to be riffles where you can unload the kids, paddle through the obvious vee pointing the way down stream, and pick up the youngsters at the bottom of the drop. Just as often, the riffle will require jumping into the water and wading through, with some dragging and hauling. A canoe trip is hardly complete without wading of some sort. Beaver dams, gravel bars or a silted estuary may call for putting on the tennis shoes and hopping in over the knees. Sometimes the exit of one person from the canoe is sufficient to provide the clearance; often it takes both. Later, your kids will get into the act. Wading canoes through shallows or minor rapids is as much a part of canoeing as slapping mosquitoes, and much more worthwhile, so be prepared for wet jeans and sneakers, and approach the inevitable with good humor.

Other river-running decisions, usually for larger rivers, involve islands and backwaters or oxbows. Generally, when the channel around an island is in doubt, the largest piece of water, and the first to make its course known, is the likely choice for the canoeist, as the smaller, less decisive fork may peter out by the time the lower end of the island is reached. Oxbows and backwaters are the result of earlier river courses, now abandoned or in the process of abandonment by a river whose rhythm and volume have changed. That same rhythm, and the hardness or softness of the terrain through which the river travels, will determine the outer limits of its course. What the canoer needs to know is that the current moves fastest and deepest at the outside of a bend and shallow and

Canoe tripping with kids

Let the kids follow the route on the map, so they can be a part of the planning and execution as well. Trip maps are between sheets of clear Contact. (Note glove and grips for handling hot pots. Two steel tubes with the ends flattened permit you to build a large fireplace and grill almost anywhere. They're easy to carry, too.)

slower at the inside. In a straight section the current runs fastest in the center and slowest at the edges. With experience, you will learn to feel the rhythm and naturally follow the most efficient route. But even the most river-wise and experienced of paddlers ends up on a gravel bar from time to time, since something wiser than physics not infrequently dictates a perverse exception to the rules.

Lake Route-Finding

The real route-finding skills will come in lake travel and the location of portages, stream inlets and outlets, or camp-sites tucked into a bay. The trip-planning process should plot a route which gives ample leeway to the family's appetite and physical capabilities. Five to ten miles a day, perhaps including a quarter-mile portage, may be an ambitious benchmark in planning for a young family on its first trip. In succeeding years one may confidently plan on ten to fifteen miles a day. A river with good current and without portages may allow for days of twenty miles or more. On the Yukon River, as an extreme example, with a seven- to ten-mile-an-hour surge and no portages for five hundred miles, eighteen hours of high-latitude day-light during mid summer allow one to cover as much as fifty miles in a single day.

On this your first major canoe trip, you have wisely chosen a chain of small lakes connected by short portages, and at least two days will be spent on rivers and creeks of a meandering nature. Your longest portages and biggest lakes are near the end of your trip when packs are lightest and your crew seasoned and fit. For smaller lakes or ponds no compass is necessary, but on larger lakes, a compass will be helpful in your dead reckoning. There is not the time or inclination for fancy calculations, triangulation or the like. You merely set the compass on the map and orient to fit. If you are heading due south and the river outlet, your destination, is judged to lie in that relation to your present position, the map will be oriented upside down in front of you. It is then a matter of identifying and determining the number of points, bays, islands, or stream inlets that will be passed as you proceed south-ward to your objective.

Even without a compass, you can easily follow this sequence. While the shortest straight-line distance may indicate a straight shot down the center of the lake, you wisely choose a course that favors the right—in this case, the western shore. As you proceed from point to point, count off landmarks from the map as each one is over-taken; three bays (*B*, *D*, and *F*), three points (*C*, *E*, and *G*), on the right, and three islands on the left. Check your navigation by looking both forward and backward as you proceed, since your perspective will be continually chang-ing as the canoe's position changes. Your course will also keep in mind the desirability of avoiding wide-open bodies of water where a sudden or changing wind may put your fleet in jeopardy. Especially with kids, it's reassuring to have a nearby shoreline to retreat to in case of a sudden squall, or in the face of mounting head winds. Depending on wind direction, points of land and islands can be used to break the wind, and your course should be plotted ac-cordingly.

In fact, wind will always be the canoeist's most perverse adversary, and many times it is preferable to stay en-camped, or ashore, until the winds drop or assume a more favorable direction. Battling headwinds can be frustrating and unproductive; better to remain in camp, write in the diary or mend the broken pack strap. Better yet, one should choose a route which takes careful con-

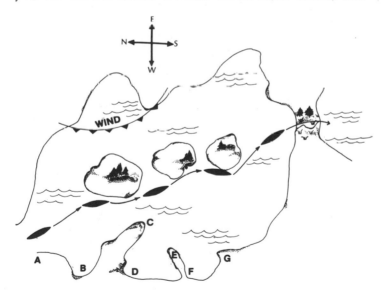

sideration of the size and orientation of the lakes. A big lake is not necessarily to be avoided, for it may be island studded, or long and narrow, oriented to be trouble-free in all but the most serious gale.

Having determined on the course, even one which may require revision as you proceed, it makes sense to communicate the general route to bow partner and crew, and

The map is spread out on the packs in front of you, oriented to the compass directions.

to point out a distant objective, such as a prominent point or a pine standing above its neighbors on a far shore.

Sometimes in the toil of making one's way, this advice is forgotten. Absorbed in your own map-reading, and intent upon an unarticulated strategy, exhilarated by a tail wind or wearied by a long day's paddle, you are oblivious to the growing resentment of your crew, who, not being privy to your deliberations, find each paddle stroke to be an unrewarding effort. Your bow paddler and crew need a goal, and with the objective in view, aching muscles are forgotten, the paddle lightens and the pace quickens. The kids, in particular, need incentives, so give them something to go for.

As the southern tip of your lake is approached, you will be conscious of a perceptible dip in the topography; a gap in the surrounding hills, where the stream, unnavigable but decisive in its course, has cut through the lowest point of land to join waters with a smaller lake beyond. Somewhat higher ground to the left of the stream outlet contrasts with the marshy tangle on its right flank, and signifies the likely location of the portage, and, sure enough, a long dead tree trunk has been swung into place by a previous party for use as an unloading dock; a blaze mark faded with years on a tattered beech tree near water's edge, and telltale, trampled-out grass announce that you have found the portage.

PORTAGING

The degree of planning and finesse of execution will vary directly with the length of the portage, but even for the shortest of carries it is best to get something into the kids' hands immediately. Even the youngest canoe trippers, if they can walk, can carry across a paddle, life preserver or tackle box.

Curious and fidgety from being too long in the canoe, the kids will likely be the first across the portage as you struggle with canoes, portage yokes, and the consolidation of packs for efficient portaging. Most portages in the actively traveled canoe areas can be safely embarked upon by the kids alone. The trails are well worn and obvious, and the roughest will be no more strenuous or demanding than the kids' favorite haunts near home. We usually caution them to step over, not on, obstacles such as logs and boulders, and impress on them the seriousness of an accident far from help. In years gone by our trail mishaps have been few and have involved nothing more serious than a skinned knee or mud-filled boot.

While a few loose items may be appropriate for employing the kids' energies, the larger folks will want to avoid any kind of hand baggage unless it is a paddle, which may be used as a walking staff. A ten-pound tackle box dangling from the end of your arm will wear you out quicker than seventy-five pounds square on the back. Tackle boxes, cameras, rods, loose jackets, cook kits, grills, axes, and shovels can be stuffed into or tied onto a pack. This is the efficient approach and one which may save you the distress of left-behind items. The objective is to reduce the number of loads and thus the number of trips across the portage. During the early years of family canoe tripping—despite a lean outfit—you will no doubt be providing porter service for young children, and will find it necessary to double or triple the portages. For a mile-long portage, that could be a distance of five miles. Good planning and realistic assessment of the family's physical capabilities are absolutely essential.

The old-fashioned Duluth packs with leather straps and tumpline are still the most effective means of portaging large quantities of food and gear, and it is perfectly satisfactory to carry more than one pack. Strength permitting, a pack on the back, with a duffel bag piled atop, is a reasonable load for all but the longest carries. If halfway down the trail you wish to lighten up, dump the second pack and pick it up on the return journey; at least you have saved yourself half a trip load. One may also hang a pack in front, but this does impede vision.

The same admonition applied to kids about "stepping over" applies to adults, too. Carrying up to 50 precent or more of one's own body weight above the waist not only affects balance, but concentrates excessive pressure on the leg pirouetting atop a barkless log or glistening boulder. There will be plenty of tests for agility in a normal day's canoeing and portaging without inviting mishap.

Getting the canoe across the portage requires some additional skill, but need not discourage you. One member of the family should master the technique of getting a canoe up and down from the shoulders, before heading off for the bush. Brawn is not called for, and the situation has improved greatly since the earlier days of waterlogged wood and canvas canoes. Lightweight aluminum canoes, seventeen feet long are under seventy pounds, and one very versatile sixteen-and-a-half-foot canoe in Kevlar capable of transporting about a half a ton, weighs under fifty pounds. I recommend that one person master the canoe carry, since the awkwardness of the two-person carry, particularly over uneven ground, has created more enemies than friends. The sharing of the weight does not seem to compensate for the aggravation of an out-of synch tango by bow and stern partners.

Portaging yokes are available, but I prefer to tie in canoe paddles, using a life preserver as padding. It gets rid of two paddles, one life preserver, and provides a broad surface on the shoulder, as well as handholds for shifting positions on a long portage. Sash cord tied in place at the outset of the trip renders this a five-minute operation at the beginning of each portage.

If the technique of rolling up the canoe from knees to shoulder eludes you, it is perfectly satisfactory to have your partner or stout youngster hold up one end of a bottom-side-up canoe, as you back under, crouching, to assume your position under the middle thwart. At the end of the carry, the canoe may either be rolled down, shoulders to knees to ground; or, by employing an accomplice to grab the bow as you crouch to rest the stern on the ground, you can walk out from under it.

Some final advice on canoe portaging. Stow all lines securely and don't tie or stuff gear into the ends of the canoe. An errant bow or stern line dragging behind may decide to grab a passing branch just as you start over a slippery corduroy of logs, or it may lasso your feet. The weight of the lightest objects in the extremity of a seventeen-foot canoe, balanced on the fulcrum of your shoulders, is magnified, creating an even more unwieldy burden. Resist the temptation to stuff odds and ends into the canoe ends; give them to the kids to carry, or better yet, get them into a pack.

It is a tall order to make a convincing argument for the

Portaging yoke.

Have a partner or stout youngster hold up one end of the canoe as you back under, crouching to assume your position under the middle thwart.

joys of portaging, but the portage should not be an object of fear or aversion. If you have organized your gear compactly, utilizing much of the light-weight equipment and foods available to the canoeist, it need not be an ordeal. The portage may in fact provide a much-needed break for kids and parents confined for several hours of lake or river paddling. Many times, the whole gang will eagerly look forward to the landfall and the thrill of new discoveries.

The end of the portage trail reveals a new vista. One of canoe tripping's most rewarding moments is the first glimpse of a new body of water, beckoning through a final curtain of trees. In the span of a portage, a sad and brooding lake, with marshy and uninviting shores, is left behind. Rising just a few feet in elevation, you find yourselves at portage-end looking down at a dazzling lake, its rocky shores punctuated at intervals with lofty cliffs. The newly discovered lake invites you to move the canoes and gear quickly over the trail, in anticipation of exploring its darkened coves and fishy depths. Three days and as many portages have put your party beyond the legions of weekend canoers. The solitude which you have sought is now at hand.

The portage trail means adventure to us; a respite from the toils of the paddle, or the monotony of a lake; anticipation of new vistas and the extension of our expeditionary status. The portage trail also brings alive the history of the area as we tread the paths which in previous centuries, and even into prehistory, bore the footprints of earlier travelers. Unlike the impersonality of the lakes and rapids, whose memory of the transient visitor is short, if not oblivious, and whose waters follow their own destinies once passed, the trail retains the prints of its makers, and by its very existence, assures us, quite literally, that we are on the right path. There is something to be gained by us and our children from walking in the footsteps of the voyageur, of Alexander Mackenzie, Peter Pond, Father Marquette, or the thousands that made the Klondike Gold Rush.

Plan your trip around the portages. They are not impediments, but links which enable us to extend our endeavor and differentiate an expedition from an excursion. They cross the divides, pay respect to the falls and cataracts, pierce the forest barrier and tell us a story in repayment for the sweat which we spill along the way, as we make our own contribution to their immortality.

CAMPSITES

Although you have selected a point-to-point canoe trip, organized to allow eight days of travel, three rest days and an insurance day, there are obviously other options. The point-to-point, including the downriver trip, may be the most satisfying, in that new scenery is maximized in the time available. It also means, however, that points of interest, once passed, cannot be revisited. Going point-to-point and coming back by the same route offers the possibility of exploring and revisiting these on the return journey. The dream campsite inevitably seen after the first mile's paddle the morning after encamping in some mosquito-infested swamp, is one you will want to identify for occupation on the return trip.

Another option is a circle trip, which, like the point-to-point, maximizes the variety of scene. Hybrids are also possible; as you retrace your inbound route, a detour circles you through some new geography and returns you to your basic route. Needless to say, the availability and choice of options are dictated largely by the geography itself, the portages, river directions, lake orientation and, of course, your own abilities.

The Base Camp

Another option which may be appealing for beginning families, or several families, or where a wide range of family wishes demand satisfaction, is the base camp strategy. Here, one seeks a large, comfortable site, offering as many indigenous attractions as possible while permitting one-day or overnight excursions on foot or by canoe. This permits the establishment of a well-organized and comfortable base where more sedentary members of the group can read, swim, sunbathe, carve, or write in their diaries, while others take off on hiking, fishing, spelunking, photography, or whitewater excursions. The peripatetic ones can return to the relative comforts of a base which, with each passing day, accretes the amenities for gracious wilderness living.

The security of the base camp is a good introduction to family canoeing, while permitting forays as ambitious as curious young appetites will embrace. A customized program can be developed for young and restless kids, who if committed for long hours to a day-after-day canoe trip might well rebel, souring both you and them on the whole idea of canoe tripping.

Your choice of a base camp is going to be of the essence; a commitment which consciously embodies all that you hope to gain from a canoeing vacation. The base-camp trip is also a provisional approach to family canoe camping, whereby an attempt is made to limit the uncertainties or opportunities for misery. Once you opt for the bolder course, which takes you and your crew further from the comforts of civilization and. subjects them to the unpredictability of the route, then you find that campsites fall into a range of expediency and choice.

Campsites of Expediency

At one extreme, winds may enforce an early encampment on the last island before you must break out into a broad sweep of lake, white-capped by winds, gusting down an uninterrupted expanse. Headway is unsafe, if not impossible, and prudence dictates that the canoes be gotten off the water. Since these surprises tend to occur as the schedule tightens, and the deadline of your rendezvous looms, a new strategy must be devised. A large mid-day meal is prepared and following that, the largest of the two tents is erected where all four of you can squeeze in and nap as best you can. The approach of dusk should bring a drop in the winds, allowing you to re-embark with the intention of putting this lake behind you. The final portage of the trip lies at the north end of the lake, and beyond is the rendezvous point. To wait until morning risks the rising winds, and the prospect of being wind-bound indefinitely.

By six-thirty the winds have died and the lake becomes quiet. With plenty of daylight left, you and your family repack the canoes and push off up the lake. Even as darkness falls, the ability to navigate is undiminished. The contours of the hills and valleys are still evident, and the islands and headlands by which you plot your course stand out, reflected in a still luminous lake.

The canoe glides quietly and swiftly over the now silent lake under a star-filled sky, and it is just before eleven o'clock that you realize the entire lake has been crossed. An occasional lantern or the still glowing embers of a dying campfire announce that others are camped, and now, in darkness, a place for the night must be found. Groping along a shoreline, you find a reasonably open and flat indentation. Clouds of mosquitoes, on their vampire rounds, torment the crew as tents are hastily erected on dark and unfamiliar terrain.

The light of day reveals a campsite that was never meant to be, and would undoubtedly have been rejected under other circumstances. But it has served its purpose well and the strategy has been successful. Most times, however, the canoeist is looking for a lot more than just a place to pitch a tent or roll out a sleeping bag.

While wind or other unpredictable circumstances may force a campsite of expediency, canoers who become too fussy about where they camp often drive their limits of choice to the point of expediency. The immutable axiom is that paddlers become fussier about their campsite in direct proportion to the lateness of the hour.

A good rule to follow is to start looking for a campsite

about three o'clock in the afternoon, and stick with the first decent one you find. If circumstances have kept your group on the water until early evening, then, by all means grab the first one you see, regardless of its imperfections. A common occurrence, particularly as more canoers take to the popular canoe highways, is to find that the campsite anticipated in the itinerary is occupied. This can be upsetting to the family arriving tired and hungry, and who for the last hour have been asking, "When are we going to . . . ?" If there is the slightest doubt about finding a campsite in the next mile, the occupants of the campsite should be queried for permission to share the campsite.

We, like others who have taken to the canoe routes for their vacation, are anxious to avoid civilization of any kind, even a single tent, but on those few occasions when we have had to share a campsite, either by our choice or the other party's, we have met the nicest and most congenial people imaginable, and what else would one expect; they're canoers like us!

Campsites of Choice

It does not take long to develop a sense about campsites. Certain shorelines, the set of the topography, the forest silhouette, or the prevailing winds will give clues as to a likely spot. The contour lines on a topographical map will also provide clues as to where *not* to camp. Low-lying or marshy areas are usually designated. Closely stacked contour lines tell you that the terrain is too steep and rocky. These are clues only, however, and many an unlikely surrounding has yielded up superior campsites.

Winds and the weather, bugs, sunsets or sunrises, fishing, hiking, swimming or just plain loafing may be the important determinant of your camping place. The breezy point, jutting into the lake, on a hot, sunny day in the height of the blackfly season may look very inviting, as the steady breezes off the lake permit you to work and play in comfort; but when the temperatures are in the fifties, and the skies are threatening, you may wish to avoid this very same place. A campsite, bright and cheery, warmed by the sun in the evening, may be dark and damp until late in the morning, when the sun finally finds it again. If an early start on the day is important to you, a campsite that will catch the morning sun is preferable. A tent snuggled deep in the woods may be refuge from winds and rain, but in the summer months, the hole in the woods is likely to come alive with hordes of mosquitoes as soon as the winds die.

The ideal campsite is near the water, but not so close as to drown in the early morning mists, or to risk rising water; it has a view, but is not unduly exposed to weather which may come up suddenly. It is open and gently rounded or sloping, not depressed; so that a heavy rain will drain away. The surrounding trees protect but do not oppress or threaten with dead branches waiting for the first good breeze to drop them on the tent. Fresh water is convenient for drinking and cooking; a sandy or rock-shelved beach invites swimming, but is not so abrupt as to invite a mishap with the kids. Fishing is nearby, and you have what seems to be an entire lake to yourself and your family. The perfect campsite does exist, but as the description suggests, compromise is inevitable. If the kids have swimming on their minds, and your Shangri-La is surrounded by fields of lily pads, you may have to re-program them for fishing.

Try to determine beforehand, from outfitter or other sources, the whereabouts and description of campsites along the route, and try, as well, to plan for alternates. Earlier comments about fussiness should be given heed, in any event, since it is not likely that you are going to find the perfect campsite. With time you will learn to develop a sense for spotting good places to camp, and just when you think you have it all figured out, you will end up having to cut your own site out of brush and weeds, employing the kids as trampers and yankers. But there's a certain satisfaction in this creation, and it may well be that a service is performed for the next hapless camper coming down the river too late in the day.

What about campsites to be avoided? You may wish to be on the lookout for obvious hazards, such as steep embankments, steep and slippery rocks near the shore, or tent sites on the edge of a bluff, but too great a preoccupation with hazards is likely to keep family canoeists at home. Every one of our kids has fallen into the drink at one time or another, and David Jr. probably holds some kind of record for partial and total immersions. It seems inevitable, so the best precaution is extra rations of dry clothes for the kids. Your kids take their fair share of chances already, walking to school or riding in the automobile with you, so don't spend too much time worrying about the health hazards likely to be found around campsites.

Those campsites that tend to be appealing to Moms and Dads will also be appealing to kids, and there is a premium on finding sites that are large enough to accommodate the sprawling nature of family activity, and also provide the options for hiking, swimming, berry-picking, fishing or historical exploration. Sometimes there is a double bonus.

On a family trip on a river in the Yukon Territories we came upon a Ninety-eighter log cabin, which, unlike others we had seen, appeared sound and habitable despite its years. Tacked on the front door was a note:

> This our home
> please do not molest
> cabin for travelers across the river.

We pushed open the door, and there was an official Gold Rush cabin, complete with bunks and a wood-burning stove. The kids were initially wary about spending the night in such an unfamiliar setting; a sway-backed, sod-roofed log cabin with a musty smell of semi-antiquity.

We talked ourselves into setting up housekeeping, including Nancy and Juli making an apple pie, now that we had a real oven. Having made our mark with this domestic activity, it was easy to accept the cabin as our home for the night, and we spread out our sleeping bags on the cots, delighted to be relieved of tent-pitching chores for the first time in almost a month.

No matter where you find your ideal campsite, try to leave it cleaner than when you found it. In those areas where the canoe traffic is heavy, one must be very careful with garbage, the fireplace, and the general debris that a small family can generate. What we can't burn, we carry out, and at each camp-breaking there is a sweep of the site, not only for litter, but also to find camping articles that seem to have little legs. "Take only pictures; leave only footprints," is a good code to live by.

Your outfitter has arrived in a cloud of dust, bringing with him the smells of civilization, reassuring but unsettling at the same time. You are all looking forward to a solid roof over your heads, and a hot shower; a dinner with salad and cold milk, and a cold beer for Mom and Dad. No need to search for the elusive, perfect campsite tonight; lumpy terrain or cooking water that must be procured with pitons and climbing rope are no longer your concern. But even as the truck goes jolting down the logging road toward town and its comforts, and, later, when you are seated at your first civilized meal in two weeks, you and your family will recall to one another the memorable bivouacs, which, with time receding, take on an even more romantic aura.

Later, after you have unpacked your gear at home and set up your tents in the backyard for a final airing and sweeping out, to be packed away for the season, the sand and forest duff, perhaps a weed or two, and a flattened, but well-preserved daddy longlegs will be all that endure to remind you of campsites now remote in distance and relevance.

11: Diversions for the kids

Forth upon the Gitche Gumee,
On the shining Big-Sea-Water,
With his fishing-line of cedar,
Of the twisted bark of cedar,
Forth to catch the sturgeon Nahma,
Mishe-Nahma, King of Fishes,
In his birch canoe exulting
All alone went Hiawatha.

Your trip plan should provide for activities other than paddling, portaging, making and breaking camp and cooking. For certain families or groups it may, in fact, be desirable to design the trip around the diversions, rather than vice versa. The base-camp strategy described in the last chapter is the ultimate vehicle for the diversion-centered trip. The other extreme is, of course, a trip which stresses maps, mileage, and points of historic or scenic interest. Goal-oriented parents need to choose the happy compromise between having fun—that's the kids' goal—and meeting a time and distance schedule. Even an aggressive schedule needs to allow for breaks.

CHORES

"Work before play." You may not be able to make all the chores fun, but they are part of the canoe tripping experience, and everybody's pitching in is essential to success. There is water to be fetched, wood to be gathered, dishes to be washed, tents to be pitched and air mattresses to be inflated. Conveying to the kids the importance of the

146

tasks, and the expectations you have about their role in making it all happen, will be the key. "Work before play!" We've heard it a thousand times before; we probably believe strongly in it; we want to pass on the ethic. The simple, but inescapable, requirements of a canoe trip provide the golden opportunity.

FISHING

Don't count on this activity to fill out your menu, otherwise it will be a chore. Fishing is probably the number one diversion of canoe trippers, and when the anglers get

The proud fisherman.

lucky, fresh fish are a great addition to the menu. Is there a kid that doesn't like to fish? Even when they are "skunked," the combination of anxiety and activity, the casting and the reeling, the fish that invariably jumps out of the water six feet beyond casting range, will keep kids absorbed for hours. Size is not important to most young kids, so if you have the choice of filling the bottom of the boat with sunfish, or stalking the depths for hours in pursuit of the wily bass, suppress your own yearnings and go for the action.

Canoe trippers should pay up for quality when shopping for a canoe and other equipment, but for occasional fishing, you should consider the very inexpensive spin-casting outfits that can be purchased in almost any sporting goods store. Canoe tripping and kids are tough on rods and reels. Unless there is a real serious fisherman in the crowd, these inexpensive outfits can be considered as disposable. Simple, inexpensive gear; a compact but comprehensive selection

If they keep 'em—they clean 'em!

The Northern Pike will strike at anything, comes in extra large sizes, and is guaranteed to give the kids a thrill.

of lures; and a schedule that allows time for exploring inviting fishing holes, make an infallible recipe for a memorable trip. Spoons and spinners are suitable lures for most fish, but consider the lowly worm. As a fish-getter, it has a good track record, too!

TRACKING

You can travel to the wildest and most thinly populated environs imaginable, and your canoeing entourage will glimpse only a fraction of wildlife that inhabits the area. Closer to civilization, it is startling to discover how much animal activity there is, but how seldom we see the creatures in the flesh.

As you canoe, rather than be disappointed at the scarcity of wildlife sighting, be alert to the many signs of their unseen presence. You and the kids can profit greatly by becoming familiar with the tracks, droppings, gnawings, scratching, rubbings, dams, nests, burrows and other evidences of animal commerce. Animals must have water, both for sustenance and enjoyment (just like humans), so the canoer probably has more opportunities to discover animal activity than any other outdoor traveler. A sandy beach or muddy river bank can yield an encyclopedia of faunal information.

Tracks are by far the most revealing source of information about creatures who traverse the soft earth, mud or dust. They can tell the expert exactly when and where the creature passed, its species, its size, its mood, whether young or old, perhaps its sex, and whether it is alarmed and fleeing for safety, or dozing in the sunshine.

But reading tracks is not easy. Just as Perry Mason seeks different clues to solve a case, the animal tracker must use ingenuity in interpreting what he sees. A track in the mud may look very different from one made in the dust, and will seldom resemble the track depicted in the guide book. The track you see may be incomplete, or may not show the imprint of all the toes, or may be misshapen because of uneven ground. There are variations due to age and sex, and very often the front track is different from the hind track of the same animal. In other words, the perfect track is seldom found.

The same applies to scats (droppings). Those of a half-grown coyote may resemble those of a young dog, and if the coyote has been feeding on bulky food, with a lot of fur or feathers, the dropping is likely to be unusually large. The droppings of an animal on a lean diet may be very small. Being accurate is not all important. Years ago, on a canoe trip in the Adirondacks of New York state, we made the acquaintance of two forest rangers, named Mel and Red. They were interested in our little canoeing adventure, and took time out to point out to our five- and

six-year-old daughters the scats and other signs of porcu-
pines. In the days that followed, and on succeeding trips,
our daughters—now woods-wise—called our attention to
every forest leaving. Anything short of a moose pie was
credited to the ubiquitous porcupine.

A fun project requiring some advanced planning is to
make a record of some of the tracks encountered on your
canoe journey. This will also be helpful in comparing and
identifying them at a later time. One method is to make
a free-hand drawing, which is good for a long series of
tracks, for faint tracks, and for bad light. Speaking of
drawings, our kids became quite adept at "drawing"
tracks in the dirt with a pointed stick. Giant bear and wolf
tracks discovered around our campsites would elicit from
us protestations of mock horror.

Tracks can be preserved in a photograph, but you may
have trouble with too much light, not enough, incomplete
tracks, faint tracks, etc. The advantage of photographs is
the possibility of including the landscape or the setting. A
third method of preserving tracks is to obtain a three-
dimensional cast, using plaster of paris. You will need
plaster of paris, a 1½-inch wide strip of cardboard (pre-cut
to about twelve inches in length), a paper clip and some
talcum powder. Mix the plaster of paris in a paper cup,
according to directions (add water and stir until it becomes creamy), form a circle with the cardboard around
the track, securing the adjoining ends with a paper clip,
sprinkle the track liberally with the talcum powder, and
pour in the plaster. After the mold has hardened, lift it out,
remove the cardboard to be used again, and wash the mold
off. You have a permanent record and proof of the monster bear; no matter that it passed by a week ago.

OTHER DIVERSIONS

The list is limitless, and for every one we have thought of,
or tried, you can probably add many more. One of the
not-so-obvious diversions is the rest-day (or rainy-day)

show. The Berton family, whom we meet on our Yukon trip (Yukon Encounter) had elevated this to an art form, employing poetry readings, singing, mimes and skits, and ghost stories. Take your pick. We have seen our own kids, and others, in ages ranging from five to seventeen, create elaborate scenarios and creative theatrics, using available props and often incorporating the agonies and ecstasies of canoe trip events. Often, the shows served to take our minds off a rainy or windbound day. But your "shows" need be nothing more than singing off key. Sometimes, in the canoes, when you and the rest of the crew are at their wits' end, for reasons of weather, fatigue or boredom, it's the time to break into song.

Take a pocket book for reading, a deck of cards, a diary and a pen. Do you remember mumb'ly peg? We watched six kids spend two hours exploiting this appalling game, a threat to both the knives and toes. Our kids have discovered steep, smooth rocks to use as a slide. They have broad-jumped, and, to our horror, cliff-jumped. Everyone enjoys a swim, and many times we have taken a spur-of-the moment plunge, to reawaken our bodies and refresh the spirit. No matter what the water temperatures, a way is found to get in the water; Mom gingerly wetting herself one drop at a time, while the seven-year-old dives into the frigid waters totally oblivious, to emerge minutes later with teeth chattering, and blue lips.

Whittling has been the refuge of the bored since time immemorial, but teach the kids how to use a knife cor-

The kids will whittle for hours.

rectly and safely before you let them loose. Craftsmanship on a small scale is fun, but how about building a raft? It takes a unique combination of downed and available timber, and lots of parent and kid power; but what makes more sense than constructing a crude, lumbering watercraft when you are surrounded by a thousand dollars worth of canoes?

We love to canoe, but sometimes we need to know what's beyond the riverbank, or what lies beyond the next

If the materials are available, try building a raft. This was built entirely of driftwood piled upon the beaches of a wilderness river. It later traveled side by side with the canoes for almost ten miles down river, before becoming hopelessly hung up on a gravel bar.

hill. Perhaps a path leads to a deserted cabin, a cave, a tiny, but fish-filled pond. Hiking side trips are a great diversion, and you can often plot out a trip route and schedule which provides for making such a detour. With the price of gold skyrocketing, give gold-panning a whirl, but remember you will need the knees of an NFL lineman and the patience of Job, and, when all your labors are done, you will be fortunate if you have found enough specks to pay for the liniment.

GOLD-PANNING

If you happen to find yourself in country where gold has been known to occur, you should be able to find a gold pan. In the Yukon they are available at most general

Panning for gold could be a profitable activity these days, but it is hard work.

stores. They come packed in a heavy grease that is best removed by burning off in the campfire (an "old timer's" superstition).

The best sites for panning placer gold deposits are found in meandering streams at the insides of the bends and downstream of large rocks—where the drop in water velocity causes the heavy gold (gold's specific gravity is the heaviest of all the elements) to be deposited.

A shovelful of steam bed materials is loaded into the pan and vigorously shaken under water to take out most of the smaller and lighter sand and gravel particles. A vigorous sloshing action is continued, to remove all but two or three tablespoons of the smallest and heaviest material. With this remaining material in the pan, scoop up some water with the tip of the pan, and with a careful rocking motion start the water slowly circulating in one direction around the bottom edge of the pan. This motion will separate the heavier from the lighter minerals—with the lighter minerals falling at the trailing edge of the material in the pan. If there is gold present, it will be on the leading edge of the sample. This dust is then collected on the fingertip and placed in a collection bottle.

I am sure we have touched on only a fraction of the possibilities for "extracurricular activities" open to canoeists. In the final chapter, we discuss the value of keeping a record on your trips in the form of a diary, photographs or movies. The serious photographer and his cast will be so intent on recording the plots and sub-plots, that they will create their own diversion.

But why diversions at all? The canoe trip itself is a diversion. We go so that we can enjoy a changed mode of life and experience, with sights and sounds that are missing from our work-a-day existence. We go to clear our minds (and perhaps our bodies) of the cobwebs, and to renew our roots with nature. We want to exist, if only for a short while, in a state of harmony with our environment—set free from the tyrannies of mechanization, released from the requirements of social and business intercourse.

The swish of the paddle, as our canoes glide through a natural amphitheater of forest and sky, the plaintive cry of the loon at dusk, and the sweet smell of new buds mingled with the odors of antiquity arising from the forest duff—here are all the diversions any person could desire.

12: Living with the inevitable

Draw a magic circle round them,
So that neither blight nor mildew,
Neither burrowing worm nor insect,
Shall pass o'er the magic circle;
Not the dragon fly, Kwo-ne-she,
Not the spider, Subbekashe,
Nor the grasshopper, Pah-puk-keena,
Nor the mighty caterpillar . . .

Our case for the wondrous experiences and manifold benefits of family canoe tripping would be even more convincing if we could show you how to draw a magic circle around your tribe to protect them from the less-appealing elements that are inevitably a part of canoe tripping. The flying, crawling variety referred to by Hiawatha are innocuous compared to the more numerous and persistent insects that await the outdoors adventurer. Add to this the vagaries of weather and the promise of hard work, and it's enough to send you back to watching the "soaps."

The first step is to accept the inevitability of intrusions in Paradise. By knowing what to expect, and reshaping your attitude, you will draw your own "magic circle." A blend of curiosity, foreknowledge, planning, and guile will put canoe tripping's goblins in their rightful place. Indeed, minor inconvenience may give way to respect, and respect to peaceful coexistence, if not exactly fast friendship.

INSECTS

Insects will be found everywhere and anywhere you venture, and, at times, certain species are so numerous as to literally drive one mad. But, insects have their habitats. It is not likely you will find a blackfly in Florida, or a scorpion in Maine. Knowing what to expect and knowing the preferred environment of certain pests may help you avoid an unpleasant experience. Let's explore their world—not as future entomologists—but to understand our adversaries.

We are going to concern ourselves with the two types of insects most troublesome to the canoer. In the interests of scientific exactitude, we shall divide them into two categories: the Biters and the Stingers. The Biters are mosquitoes, no-see-ums, chiggers, ticks, spiders and several types of flies. The Stingers are wasps, hornets, bees and scorpions.

Biters

Mosquitoes (family Culicidae). There is no question but that the mosquito was invented to teach canoers humility. No visitor to the North Woods can fail to be impressed by their numbers and persistence. Every locale has story-tellers vying to impress upon their listeners the superiority in numbers, voraciousness, or wingspan of their own native population. Alaskans brag more about their mosquitoes than they do about their oil. Judge Wickersham, one of the first of his profession to set up a frontier bench in the Territory, devotes a chapter in his memoirs to the omnipresent hordes. In one wry passage, he describes a meal accompanied by hard and unyielding biscuits, and notices at first his pleasure that the cook has thoughtfully embellished them with currants. On closer examination, the currants turn out to be mosquitoes.

The Judge's sense of humor would be worth your while to imitate in dealing with mosquitoes. Everyone recognizes the pest, but did you know that only the female can bite?

The next time you are besieged by a million or more mosquitoes, there may be some consolation in knowing that only half of them can bite. The males are equipped with a rudimentary mouth and cannot bite, while the female is blessed with a long proboscis especially designed for sucking. And, for a reason: the female mosquito needs a blood meal in order to lay its eggs.

The eggs are laid on standing water, singly, or in floating, raft-like masses. The larvae (the second stage all insects go through) are humpbacked little wigglers. If you stir up some still water, you can spot them wiggling around. Mosquitoes and their progeny thrive in wet or marshy environments, and seem to have an aversion to wind and sunlight. You should choose your lunch stops and campsites with that in mind.

There are times, however, when you just have to contend with mosquitoes. Early morning and dusk definitely bring an increase in their activity, which is regulated in a daily cycle by the hours of dark and light changing within the boundaries of twenty-four hours. The "pop" psychology about biorhythms is an extension of the application of the circadian or daily cycle of body processes and activities, suggesting that we are now discovering what the mosquitoes have known all along.

On the portage trail mosquitoes have a way of finding their way under your canoe, attracted to all the places that your unoccupied hand—if you have one—can't quite reach. Fortunately, the chemists have recently come up with some very effective potions (high in N-Diethyl-meta-toluamide, or "Deet") which are not unpleasant to apply, and which permit you to carry on your activities with relative impunity. Judge Wickersham never had a chance, and as recently as ten years ago, we had to rely on some pretty noxious and not terribly effective repellents.

The *No-see-um* (of the genus Culicoides). This miserable miniature is as minute as its name suggests, but it packs a real wallop. Its bite has been described by its admirers as being like a hot spark. The smallest of the bloodsuckers, only four one-hundredths of an inch long, the no-see-um can pass through all but the finest bug netting. Its bite usually leaves a red welt, which can keep you itching well into the night. Generally found in the more northern states and Canada, no-see-ums are most active in the morning and evening. The high-Deet repellents work on these guys, too.

Like the mosquito, the no-see-um is found near water. Their larvae, eggs, and pupae are usually aquatic, although they can be found in decomposing vegetable matter, under bark and fallen leaves, and in the sap flowing from a wounded tree.

Blackfly (family Simulidae). One outdoor writer, bewailing the bugs, was convinced of a conspiracy between the mosquito and the blackfly, whose numberless legions took turns assailing the luckless camper. In fact, there are times of the year in certain locales where respite from the early morning assaults of the mosquito are followed by the explosive eruption of the more diurnal blackfly.

Seasoned outdoorsmen actually hold the blackfly in greater abhorrence than the mosquito. It is an interesting fellow, however. The blackfly is smaller than his cousin, the house fly; he is black in color, hump-backed, fast moving, hard working, gregarious, and a fierce biter. Fortunately, blackflies are prevalent mostly in the months of May and June, depending how far north you are, and start to diminish as the summer wears on.

Like the mosquito, only the female blackfly bites. However, under battlefield conditions this is neither useful nor consoling information. But let your scientific curiosity override narrow prejudices and yearnings for civilized comforts. The blackfly breeds in moving water. If you dip a white plate or a piece of paper in a fast-flowing stretch of water in blackfly country during the early summer months, you can watch the dark-colored larvae become visible against the white background. The birth of the blackfly and its escape from the rushing water into the air rivals Houdini. During the last part of the pupal stage, its skin becomes inflated with air (extracted from the water) just before the magic moment. The skin splits along the back, and a small bubble of air quickly rises to the surface and bursts, ejecting the fly into the air.

The blackfly may be a fascinating performer, if you are an entomologist, but to the canoe tripper it is a vicious, hardy adversary, which will swarm and attack en masse. Humans are not their only target. They can stampede a herd of caribou and drive a moose insane.

Avoiding the woods in May and June in certain locales is one strategy for evading the blackfly, but you should check with available sources. The further north you travel, the shorter the summer season, but nature has diabolically compensated by making the northern blackfly hordes even more numerous. In arctic latitudes, each footstep raises them in clouds from the tundra, so thick at times, that ingestion of the flies through mouth and nose and their maniacal crowding into other orifices, are more of a problem than bites.

A breeze tends to discourage these fellows too, so try to stay in the open if you find yourself in blackfly country in season. When they start to swarm, you may have to den up in your tent. If you must be out, dress for it. For the most severe conditions, a head-net, which you can tuck into your shirt, is the answer (usually a hat with netting attached). Persistent beyond belief, swarming or single blackflies will crawl about until they find the chink in your clothing armor, crawling inside hat bands, up sleeves and pant legs. They love to get behind the ears and to root around under your hair, along the hair line. In addition to using your insect repellent liberally, keep your sleeves down, and buttoned, and tuck your pant legs into your boots or socks. Light-colored clothing is preferable to dark.

Once it has found its mark, the blackfly takes a small piece of meat out of you. It is a painless operation, but often draws a spot of blood. One or two is a badge of courage, but many bites and little cakes of blood invite scratching and infection. Kids are particularly prone to scratching uncontrollably. In extreme cases, a well-chewed camper can have a very unpleasant reaction. On a trip in northern Quebec, one of our daughters stripped to swim on a "nice sandy beach," only to be attacked a few minutes later when the wind dropped. Shortly thereafter, little Juli's eyes were swollen shut. We gave her some antihistamine and she was fine by morning. In less dire circumstances, you can apply topically a good analgesic–anesthetic gel or cream, to both heal and soothe.

As forbidding as this sounds, you should not allow the blackfly to deter you in your plans. Ninety percent of the places you choose to go will not present the extremes described here, but like so many other parts of this game, knowing what to expect and time-tested defensive maneuvers will provide a tolerable co-existence.

Other Flies. Now you must watch out for the horsefly, the green headed monster, and deerflies *(Tabanidae).* Only the females bite, while the males content themselves with sipping sweets from the flowers. Unlike the blackfly or the mosquito, these other biters rarely travel in swarms. Their modus operandi is to buzz infuriatingly, dodging, darting, waiting for an opening. They love the hair, but will settle for any exposed flesh. These flies are seemingly undeterred by most bug repellents, and your only defense is to wait for the enemy to land, and then smash it! Your timing must be perfect, since they often bite on contact. They seem to prefer sunny, open areas. On an otherwise pleasant and broad portage, they delight in striking when your hands are full. These three flies, which range in size from a 747 (the horsefly) to a DC-9 (the little green heads), are an annoyance, from time to time, but hardly in the class of the mosquito and blackfly. You can swat a million of the latter with only marginal satisfaction, but felling one fat deerfly is as satisfying as a good sneeze.

Ticks and Chiggers (superfamily Ixodoidea *and family* Trombiculidae). These are found mostly in the South and Southwest, and along the east coast. The tick is the more

Canoe tripping with kids

widespread of the two, a nonflier, which will attach itself to a person brushing against woodland foliage. The tick digs in with its head, takes a small draught of blood, and leaves a swelling and a sore. Upon retiring, you should check your hair and your kids', as well as the inside of your clothing. If you find any of these hitchhikers embedded in the skin, apply a drop of kerosene, alcohol, gasoline, or grease to cut off its air supply. A quicker and equally effective treatment is to give the tick a "hot foot" with a lighted match. It will pull out fast. If the tick is embedded too deeply, it should be carefully removed with tweezers. After removing the tick, wash the bite with soap and water and treat with an antiseptic.

A chigger, another non-flier, is slightly larger than a no-see-um, and will give a sharp bite resulting in an irritating itch that may last for several days. Scratching can lead to infection, so one should get some analgesic–anesthetic gel on the bites as quickly as possible. Long sleeves, long pants, and boots—especially on the portage trail—along with plentiful bug repellent are the best defense.

Spiders. These are not insects, since they have four pairs of legs, no wings, and the head and thorax are merged into one piece. They also have eight eyes—comforting, isn't it? In the northern climates there seem to be an abundant variety, including the ever-present daddy longlegs, but none represents a problem for canoe trippers. In the South, however, painful bites can be inflicted by the tarantula, the black widow and the brown recluse, the latter two being potentially fatal to a small child. These are distinctive spiders and can usually be spotted before they cause trouble. You should know where they are likely to be found, and the kids should be taught to identify them.

Stingers

Wasps and Bees. These stingers are social insects, with the exception of some wasps, as differentiated from solitaries, such as scorpions. In a colony of social insects, one female, or queen, does most, or all, of the egg-bearing, and the un-mated females—the workers—do most of the work.

Wasps like to nest on low-hanging branches, but they rarely sting unless disturbed. Bees and yellow jackets build their nests in the ground, in logs or in hollow trees, and fast movement or a perceived intrusion can attract airborne defenders. If you spot a nest, or bee or wasp activity, avoid the area and move away slowly.

Scorpions. Scorpions are not insects, but belong to the class of spiders. They have distinctly segmented abdomens and a tail-like hind end. They are found mostly in the Southwest, and are given to crawling into shoes, boots or folds in the clothing at night. Be sure the crew investigates each item of clothing and footwear carefully before putting it on in the morning.

REMEDIES

Seeing all these devils and their potential inflictions listed in one place might discourage you. We maintain, however, that one puts up with more harassment and greater jeopardy in traffic than on an insect-plagued canoe trip; and unlike traffic, canoe tripping has some solid rewards. In spite of knowing what to expect, and all your precautions in the woods, there's a good likelihood that someone in your group will be bitten or stung. In some cases, it will be only a minor annoyance. For more serious reactions, there are good anti-sting, anti-inflammatory, analgesic, anesthetic, and antihistamine medications on the market. Check with your physician and be sure to include them in your first-aid kit.

Several "home remedies" are also possible. Cold water will help reduce swelling, as well as numb the pain of an insect bite or sting. Cool mud is especially good for bee and wasp stings, and a paste of sodium bicarbonate is quite effective for all stings and bites.

SNAKES

If you are traveling in snake country, be sure that you and the children can identify and recognize poisonous species, as well as their most likely habitats. Carry a snakebite kit and read the directions before the trip so that it can be used quickly and effectively. You should be familiar with the types of snake poison and the specific treatment for each type. Where poisonous snakes are a known hazard, you may think twice about taking young kids, but in the northern latitudes, at least, they are almost nonexistent. This statement notwithstanding, you should make yourself aware of local exceptions, for example, the sagebrush country of eastern Washington state.

RAIN

This section might also be entitled "how to stay dry." If you start with the assumption that you and your crew are going to be rained on, you will have this inevitable element partially licked. There are very few canoe tripping activities that need to be interrupted or altered by showers or rain—unless there is an honest-to-goodness downpour or a storm-driven rain. The latter, of course, means wind, and that's another kind of problem.

"Rain, rain, go away; come again another day," is a little ditty we may all have sung at one time or another. It takes on new meaning if you have suffered seven straight days of rain on a two-week trip, causing even the hardiest spirits to flag. Despite great care in planning, choosing the driest month of the year, based on mean average rainfall statistics, or choosing an area reputed to receive over three hundred days of sunshine a year, it happens; particularly if you plan to be out for more than two or three days.

What's the strategy? One option is to den up in the tent and wait out the storm. However, we have made several trips where such a tactic might have resulted in our being in camp yet! Think about being cooped up with a couple of fidgety kids for a few days! Our approach is as follows: If it isn't blowing a gale or whipping up whitecaps on the water, if progress can be made safely without fighting headwinds or chilly temperatures, and if there is no thunder or lightning, then waterproof the gang, pack up the canoes and make the mileage for the day. If progress on the water appears hazardous, get out of the tent anyway and go fish from shore, take a hike, gather dry firewood, or set up a shelter with the rain tarp (carried for this purpose).

A rain tarp is just that; a square or rectangle of coated nylon or polyethylene, ten feet by ten feet or larger, with grommets in each corner and at intermediate points. The tarp can be stretched between trees, extra tent poles, or tree limbs out of the woods, to create a stand-up shelter. The integrity of the entire structure depends on liberal use of nylon line or sash cord. Deficiency of architectural knowhow is compensated for by using plenty of cord,

The kids stay dry under a makeshift rain shelter, using a canoe as a windbreak, tarps, and lots of nylon line. The Noatak River, Alaska.

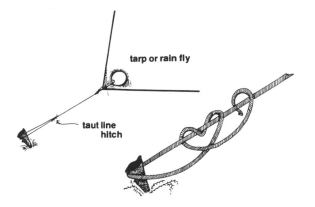

tarp or rain fly

taut line hitch

securing corners and sides with taut line hitches. A well-placed canoe paddle may be needed to prop up a strategic point or to keep a puddle from forming.

The rain shelter becomes an absorbing family project, during which the rain may be forgotten, and, when completed, it results in a psychological lift and physical comfort; a place to wait out the storm, enjoy your meal, do the cooking, and keep the packs dry.

If you are going to fish or hike, clothing becomes all important. A full rainsuit and a hat and rubber-bottomed boots will permit you to go about these activities undaunted. Rain pants are particularly important, if you are going to be sitting in a canoe for any length of time. In the woods, it is usually the water hanging on the trailside shrubbery that douses you, rather than the stuff that's falling.

Packing up a wet tent is an unpleasant prospect, but it is not going to travel far in that condition, so no harm is caused. In a few hours there is a good chance you will be setting it up again in rainless conditions, especially if the signs at the time of breaking camp encouraged you to pack up and go. The tent usually dries out within the hour. (If it happens to be the last day of your trip, however, make sure you dry the tent thoroughly before putting it back into storage.) If your other gear is packed as we have suggested in our equipment chapter, it should stay dry. Three branches, one or two inches in diameter, and the extra canoe paddle, laid lengthwise in the bottom of the canoe, will serve to keep the packs off the bottom and out of the puddle that even a light rain will create.

What happens when the gear or clothes get wet, despite your best-laid plans? Never miss an opportunity to rig up a clothesline to grab even an hour's break in a persistent wet-weather pattern. Drying over a fire has its uses, but don't rush the process, or leave unattended items in front of, or over the fire. Kids are adept at burning up socks and sneakers, so supervise them closely.

Although the gear in your packs may stay secure and dry during a prolonged rain, wet pants, socks and shoes are oft-times unavoidable. Canoers, big and small, can find ways to get wet in dry weather, too. The immediate inclination is to dig out a dry replacement, which is fine if the rain has ended for the forseeable future, and if the wet clothes can be dried soon. In either case, it is often prudent, if temporarily uncomfortable, to let these items dry while still on you. All too often, a rush to change into the dry duds results in two pairs of wet pants or sneakers, rather than one.

WIND AND WEATHER

As we have said many times, wind is the canoeist's greatest adversary. Except on small, tree-protected rivers, it can bring progress to a standstill. Canoes can be stopped dead in their tracks by wind, even in the midst of long, vigorous rapids. On lakes headway becomes impossible and, if the canoeing party is far from shore, the situation may become perilous. Wind in combination with wet can bring great discomfort, and, in the extreme, could cause or exacerbate hypothermia.

No destination or objective is important enough to keep you on the water in a high wind. Find shelter on a lee shore, or in the protection of a natural windbreak, such as a cliff, boulder, or grove of trees. If none of those is available, arrange the canoes and packs to form a windbreak. Sit it out until the wind dies. If it persists, make plans for setting up a camp which also makes use of natural or contrived windbreaks. Your fire or stove, once started, must be sheltered, since too much wind will cause the heat to dissipate before it can do its work. Dig into an embankment, or rig a rain tarp as a lean-to. Should you resort to extreme measures in getting a fire started, great care must be exercised later to be sure that the site is thoroughly soaked and the fire is dead out. The rain may cease and the wind continue. A stump, or tree roots, can burn undetected—in fact, underground—to burst forth long after you and your party have vacated.

Winds are often a concomitant of storms. They may also signal a change in the weather, heralding the end of a clear spell, as the barometer falls and a low-pressure system replaces a high. The leading edge of the new system is known as the isotherm, and suggests a change in the temperature as well. Wind may also signal the arrival of a high-pressure or clearing system, and that's good news.

Learning to read the skies and clouds, the significance of changing wind directions, whether wind is backing or veering, and the rise and fall of the barometer, can be a fascinating aspect of the canoeist's experience. Like sca-

A nose for changing weather is a good ally on a canoe trip.

farers, we are ever subject to the vagaries of the weather. The very success of our trip may depend on our ability to respond to its whims. We are always in full view of, and subject to, all the changes in weather conditions. Time and experience sharpen our senses to recognize changes. The heightened odor of the forest, the activity of birdlife, or campfire smoke that lingers like smog above our campsite, may all be signals of a low barometer, belying the comfort taken from cloudless skies. It may be the time to put the packs well under cover for the night and to check the guy lines on the rain fly.

A freshening breeze, as the winds veer from northwest to west, campfire smoke which spirals straight upward and disappears in the pine boughs above may encourage us that the 3 A.M. shower which disturbed our dreams was local and temporary. Low clouds scudding overhead may soon lift and be carried off beyond the horizon, leaving the crew basking in sunshine. The weather is not to be feared or cursed; it must be accommodated. Learning to recognize its signals, and to appreciate the complex interplay of numerous factors—some of which may be surprisingly local, and some of which may be driven by atmospheric disturbances many thousands of miles away—will make you a better canoeman and outdoorsman, while enhancing the comfort and safety of you and your comrades.

HARD WORK

It has been our intention to emphasize the pleasurable and healthful aspects of family canoe tripping. Yet a common reaction of persons discovering we have spent our vacation on a canoe trip is that that is no vacation at all. It is the same reaction many people have to cross-country skiing. Either activity is seen as a form of self-inflicted hardship or arduous physical effort.

There is a saying to the effect that people die of boredom, never from hard work. Hard work, however, must be satisfying. Knowledge and experience can reduce the amount of work required to accomplish a given task, and can ensure that the work performed is effective, rather than nonproductive. Efficient paddling technique, carefully planned portages, well-executed route-finding, nourishing food, and effective bug repellents will ensure that the canoers will work less hard to accomplish their objective.

It all comes down to planning. If individuals wish to test the limits of their endurance and skill, and if their desire is founded on solid experience and realistic assessment of the project undertaken, they may embrace hard work as play. Others may plan a trip and daily regimen that permits many hours of relaxation and time to contemplate the scene—or ignore it.

Regardless of the activity, if you enjoy it, it is not hard work—to you. Adventurers pinned down in their tent by wind and rain, find it hard work to stay in the tent, twitching for the moment when they can be off. You may welcome the same excuse to write leisurely in your diary or read the Gothic novel tucked in the side pocket of your pack for such occasions.

Pressed for time, expeditioners see cooking as a labor of necessity, to be dispatched as quickly as possible. Other canoe trippers will carry an extra fifty pounds of grub across the lake and portage; then stop to make camp at 2:30 P.M., in order to indulge in their first love, creating a gourmet feast out of doors. The same paddler who claims he has reached the limit of his physical capacity, as river bend follows river bend, endlessly, is galvanized into action after dinner; organizing a marshmallow cooking contest and then telling ghost stories to wide-eyed kids, until one by one they sneak off to their tents to seek repose. Could he find an audience, the storyteller would continue far into the night.

Some hard work is inevitable. The unexpected can and does occur. Plan for it, or plan around it. It is nothing to fear, and oftentimes you are surprised at the work capacity of kids. The same ones that regularly shirk the dinner dishes at home become veritable sherpas on the portage trail. If a good hot meal depends on it, they will range throughout the forest to bring back the necessary firewood. No matter what level of effort is planned for or experienced, everyone returns from a canoe trip with a heightened sense of well-being, a feeling of greater strength and vitality. In most cases we become reacquainted with the pleasures of hard work, especially as a result of doing something we truly enjoy.

13: For the record

Such as these the shapes they painted
On the birch-bark and the deer-skin;
Songs of war and songs of hunting,
Songs of medicine and of magic,
All were written in these figures,
For each figure had its meaning,
Each its separate song recorded.

We have touched throughout the book upon the value and satisfaction to be derived from researching and planning your canoe trip. There are even greater rewards to be had from keeping your own historical record.

Our family trip to the Yukon Territories (see next chapter) was built upon the historical record compiled by others, and if for some reason we had never been able to take the trip, we would have still enjoyed a worthwhile journey of discovery and learning. Fortunately, we were able to take both journeys.

Whether your canoe trip carries you to the Yukon, or the Ozarks, or to a nearby waterway, the canoeing environment is a great backdrop for the family chronicle. There is a minimum of contrivance in the wilderness setting and a natural empathy between the beauty of the outdoors and kids. A photographic or written journal fixes them in time and place. Hiawatha understood this well.

In twenty years of family canoeing we have amassed an extensive photographic and diary record, in addition to voluminous correspondence, brochures, maps, trip notes (ours and others'), magazine clippings, and bibliographies. A canoe trip worth taking is worth recording.

THE DIARY

If movies or photography intimidate you, settle for a small spiral pad and ballpoint pen. Diligence in the daily recording of events will ensure the success of your chronicle. The penalties for procrastination are severe, however. It is amazing how much is forgotten out of an action-packed day as time recedes. Lacking a diary, by the time the expedition returns to suburbia, numerous events and, indeed, whole days are forever lost.

An hour each evening, or early in the morning, should be set aside for the diary. For some reason, stretched out in my sleeping bag, propped up on the elbows for a dawn recording, my fingers go dead alseep, which is an impetus to both brevity and a daily routine. Doing your diary in the evening avoids this, but may conflict with setting camp, dinner, dishwashing or darkness.

There's much to be said for both husband and wife keeping a diary. In our case, one partner tends to produce a dry, factual account—one might even say dull—while the other involves the spirit world, philosophic discourse and sentimentality, producing a journal quite readable in the original.

We have also tried with varying success to get our kids to keep a diary. Those few fragments that have survived to the present are humorous for their lack of resemblance to the parental perspective on the same event. What we do learn from these shards is that the kids are preoccupied —as we suspected—with food and the weather. Subtleties of experience seem to come with age!

THE MOVIES

No question about it, movies are fun. They can capture the spontaneity of activities and the sequential event. With a zoom lens and automatic exposure control one has only to "point and shoot" to record the kids setting up tent, landing a fish, or starting off down the portage. The zoom magnification brings wildlife into closer range. From pre-trip packing, to put-in to take-out, movies can record the story, with emphasis on the action rather than one magic moment.

The seeming ease of point-and-shoot cinematography is deceptive, however, and many a home movie audience has become seasick trying to follow over-panned, super-zoomed flicks. The movie camera should be held absolutely still, just as with a still camera. Panning a movie camera (following the action or surveying a scene by moving the camera in an arc) requires a steady hand and should be done sparingly. It is far better to stop the camera, reframe the subject or action, and restart, letting the action take place within an unwavering frame.

The key to good movies is lots of footage and aggressive editing, which is obviously expensive and time-consuming. Those unwilling to invest in an editor (two film-winders and a viewing screen) and splicer, or unwilling to take the time, would be better off in another medium. Each scene should be given ample time to unfold, but assiduous editing will relieve viewers from watching two minutes of bacon frying. It takes a courageous editor to snip several feet of prime moose frames into the wastebasket, but even a moose gets dull after a couple of thousand frames.

STILL PHOTOGRAPHS

One need not invest in an expensive camera for recording the family canoe trip. The still pictures for our Yukon River adventure were recorded with black-and-white film and two Instamatic cameras. These will not produce Ansel Adams imagery, but we have a complete album of sharp snapshots which tell of the many events and scenes; daughter Juli panning for gold in Brittania Creek, Dave Jr. showing off a ten-pound Inconnu, a sod-roofed cabin in the fireweed, and a rain-soaked crew gathered around the cooking fire. Our Christmas card that year shows the family on the front stoop of Dawson City's Palace Grand, attired in flannel shirts and long dresses for the girls, carried five thousand miles for just this purpose. Our photographer was an accommodating bulldozer driver working on a nearby project.

We chose the black-and-white, snapshot format in preference to slides, since it permitted us to set up an album with appropriate captions, a coffee table conversation piece, which we and guests could thumb through at leisure. This satisfies the natural urge to "show and tell," without imprisoning your friends in a full-scale production.

With today's quality films and a well-designed Instamatic camera, one can produce a remarkably good picture, but a steady camera is essential. The extremely light 110 cameras, in particular, invite shaky operation and a finger over the lens. A practice roll shot and developed before the trip, giving attention to a slow, steady shutter release, can make the difference between visually pleasing prints or a wastebasket full of hazy rejects.

Color slides with a 35 millimeter camera, which fill the screen, can be an exciting way to bring your canoe trip back to life. Slower-speed film, such as Kodak 64, will give you brilliant colors, but offers limited flexibility in low-light or fast-action situations. High Speed Ektachrome (ASA 200) is probably the most satisfactory film for the canoer's environment.

Slides are considerably less expensive to develop than prints, so it makes sense to use rolls of thirty-six exposures and to take as many pictures as possible. As with the movies, aggressive editing is called for. Often, I will take several different exposure settings for the same scene, fully expecting to come up with discards. On the subject of exposure, the water that is often the backdrop to the family canoeing scene poses special problems. Reflected light can cause your meter to register a one- to two-stop smaller aperture (or faster speed) than is appropriate for your subject—a canoe in the rapids, for example. Opening the lens at least a stop from that indicated should avoid silhouetted or darkened canoers on a glaring white river.

For all types of pictures, morning and evening light gives a dramatic effect to your photos, when shadows and contrast are increased by the low altitude of the sun. Portraits of your family taken in the last glow before sunset can light up their faces at the time, and later your screen or album. This is true for both color or black and white.

With time, the canoeing photographer becomes more concerned about composition and imagery. The silhouette of the pines, a gurgling brook, or the symmetrical curves of the canoes may be the themes. In a favorite picture of mine, the eye-pleasing bow of the canoe points the way, as a retreating boy, rod in hand, disappears across the beach.

Luck is important too. My wife, who would readily admit to inadequacies as a photographer, captured at the edge of an Adirondack lake our five-year-old daughter's little friend, unaware of the camera, intently removing a fishhook from the seat of her pants. Having a camera ready at hand, and being alert to opportunities may make you even luckier.

Close-ups of rain-bedraggled children, or the mealtime face contorted by a "Yuk," are good reminders that all is

In search of the wily fish.

not woodsy tranquility. You will need these humorous recollections, because they are somewhat less so in the experiencing.

WATERPROOF AND READY

Keep your camera ready, preferably in a separate waterproof bag or box. The film, exposed and unused, should be kept in its own plastic or waterproof container. Don't forget to carry extra batteries.

After many years without mishap, I paid the price of complacency. I was paddling with my father-in-law, followed by my son and his companion in a second canoe. Granddad and I swept around a sharp bend where the swift current carried us into the undercut bank. A protruding root gave the canoe a jolt sufficient to knock us overboard. On the floor of our swamped canoe was my wide-open, waterproof Phoenix camera bag. I had failed to take my normal precaution of fastening up the camera bag moments earlier, after some shots of the boys fishing under the drooping rain forest canopy. My cherished Nikkormat went to the bottom of the Humptulips River, and was there for fifteen minutes until I was able to recover it. Carefully dried in the sun that afternoon, miraculously it works to this day. I am told, however, that this is exceptional, and that it is only a matter of time before some small corroded part will freeze up the entire works.

Recalling something read somewhere, I put the exposed film, now water soaked, into a juice pitcher, and kept it immersed until I could get it home and into a developing tank. Thus were preserved three generations of canoeists, reunited on a rain forest river. Barely discernible watermarks on the prints are a reminder of the mishap.

BE DILIGENT

Whether you record your trip with diary, movies, or photos, it is important to make a commitment at the outset of your trip. Planning for the recording of your

178

adventure should be given the same attention as food and equipment. Too often, the press of time or the arduous nature of the undertaking provide a convenient excuse for leaving the camera encased or allowing the journal to lapse. When you are lining a canoe through a rapid, up to your waist in water, late in the day and miles from your camp for the night, digging out the camera, to the inevitable groans of the crew, requires fortitude.

Discipline and an eye for posterity will ensure that the little adventures which make up the canoeing experience are not lost, but preserved for a later resurrection, when the winter days have shortened and the city is busy about you. Whether preparing for your trip of a lifetime, or reliving it, the time spent on research and keeping the record will reward you and your family long after the packs and paddles have been put away.

14: Yukon encounter

Tell us now a tale of wonder,
Tell us of some strange adventure,
That the feast may be more joyous
That the time may pass more gaily
And our guests be more contented!

As an illustration of the rewards of research for canoe trippers, we'll recount how an inspiration in the form of a book set the wheels in motion for our planning and realization of the ultimate family canoe trip. The book, loaned to me by a friend, was entitled *Klondike*, and was written by Pierre Berton, one of Canada's most popular authors. For reasons we were yet to learn, the book was a special labor of love for Berton.

READING UP

We were enthralled by Berton's lavish descriptions of the last, great Gold Rush, which lured an estimated 250,000 persons to the inhospitable trails leading to the gold fields. Only a fraction of those who started on the quest were successful in finding their way to Dawson City at the mouth of the Klondike River, and most were bitterly disappointed. They scaled deadly glaciers, forded icy rivers, went by mule, wagon, raft, shank's mare, and pure grit. By the time most of them arrived in the diggings, the best claims had been staked out, either by those who arrived earlier, or who were smarter. For many it did not matter.

To have made the quest, to have achieved the goal, was the real Mother Lode. Most of the so-called stampeders came away sadder but wiser; in some cases they were fulfilled. They had briefly glimpsed the muddy streets of Eldorado, and would return to families, desks, and jobs left impetuously two years earlier.

The Chilcoot Trail and the upper Yukon took most of the traffic of the Gold Rush, at least of those who were successful, but there were many more routes, by water and overland, over which the stampeders attempted to make their way to the gold fields. If the Chilcoot was harsh, there were other routes that were heart-breaking, or outright deadly. Imagine a group clawing their way across the immense and terrifying Malaspina Glacier. Of one party of about one hundred men who were landed at its base in the spring of 1898, forty-one died trying to reach the Klondike. Writes Berton, "All who survived rued the day they had ever heard the word 'Klondike'."

Other routes, some of which were touted by unscrupulous promoters in "gateway" cities such as Seattle and Edmonton (Alberta), proved to be almost as harsh. One of the Edmonton routes, however, had as its downhill portion a run of several hundred miles down the Pelly River, flowing westward from the Rocky Mountain cordillera and joining up with the Yukon for another 250 miles of river travel to Dawson.

That was the route our family chose. We would travel almost 3500 miles from our New Jersey home, by car, train, and plane to reach Whitehorse, the largest town in the Yukon Territories. From here, we required a five-hour truck portage to our put-in on the Pelly River. We were a month on the river, and landed in Dawson City on September 1, in eighty-degree weather. The trip down the Yukon culminated a voyage which had been a full year in the planning and preparation, and included the reading of several books in addition to Berton's. Three days on the train to Edmonton, Alberta—outward bound—caught us up on our bibliography.

THE TRIP

Our crew, consisting of Judy and me, our two daughters, eleven and twelve, and Dave Jr., seven, were tucked into two seventeen-foot aluminum canoes, rented in Whitehorse. We had been on the heavily silted Pelly for ten days before emerging at the confluence with the Yukon. Presiding over the junction was Fort Selkirk, a Hudson's Bay Post founded by Robert Campbell in 1848.

We were welcomed by sailor-hatted Indian, Danny Roberts, with his wife and daughter, the sole inhabitants of Fort Selkirk. Until a few years ago the post seemed doomed, as most of the buildings had started to deteriorate beyond repair. The final blow had been struck in the late 1950s, after the highway had been built through Pelly Crossing and the steamers had ceased to operate on the Yukon. Apparently a reprieve was granted by the Canadian Historical Sites Commission, however, as we found Fort Selkirk a very attractive but rustic setting.

After a quick tour of the ghostly, quasi-restoration of Taylor and Drury's emporium and dry goods establishment, the R.C.M.P. (Mounties) headquarters, a schoolhouse littered with 1908 Vancouver newspapers, and a rough-hewn church, we decided that we would camp here, breaking away for the first time from our pattern and two weeks of wilderness campsites. What a fortunate choice it turned out to be.

As I was returning from wood-chopping chores, I heard Judy, who was not visible below the high river embankment, talking with a stranger. Arriving at the edge of the embankment, I saw four large motorized rubber rafts below, out of which swarmed a host of men, women, and children. Conversing with Judy like a long lost friend was "Skip" Burns, a man with red hair dressed in blue rain chaps. Skip was a guide and outfitter for excursions out of Skagway. Gesturing at the new arrivals, he asked if we had heard of Pierre Berton, television talk show personality

Canoe tripping with kids

and noted Canadian author. Our reaction could not have been more enthusiastic.

As luck would have it, Berton was on his way to Dawson City for Discovery Days, having retraced with his family and entourage the famed Chilcoot Trail over which his grandfather had labored at the height of the stampede in 1898. Pierre Berton, himself, was born in Dawson. In Dawson, Berton would be kicking off a new edition of *Klondike*.

That evening, after all had finished dinner, a cosmopolitan group, including Danny Roberts and his wife, Abby, and Red McHugh, a late arrival from Whitehorse, gathered around the Berton's bonfire for Fort Selkirk's social event of the season, as Pierre, his wife Janet, and their seven children gave a party complete with singing, skits, storytelling, and finally a stirring recitation, by Berton himself, of "The Shooting of Dan McGrew," which resonated off

Pierre Berton recites "Dangerous Dan McGrew" for a cosmopolitan gathering at Fort Selkirk.

the basaltic cliffs opposite the fort. We sat enthralled—
our own kids wide-eyed—under the flickering stars, oblivious to the steadily dropping temperatures.

It was a once-in-a-lifetime coincidence; one family on
a pilgrimage over Grandfather Berton's trail to Dawson;
another on a pilgrimage inspired by the man whose book
had made the Gold Rush come alive.

There were exceptional rewards on the Yukon, as a
whole bibliography came alive, but those same rewards
are available, as well, to a weekend expedition on the
Delaware and Raritan Canal, in the Quetico, or anywhere
that the waters flow.

OUR YUKON READING LIST

BERTON, PIERRE. *Klondike: The Last Great Gold Rush,
1896–1899.* McClelland and Stewart, Ltd., Toronto, 1972.
(earlier edition published in U.S. by Alfred Knopf as
The Klondike Fever)

———. *Drifting Home.* McClelland and Stewart, Ltd., Toronto, 1973.

MATTHEWS, RICHARD. *The Yukon.* Holt, Rinehart & Win-
ston, New York, 1968.

PAGE, ELIZABETH. *Wild Horses and Gold; from Wyoming
to The Yukon.* Farrar & Rinehart, New York, 1932.

SERVICE, ROBERT. *Collected Poems of Robert Service.* Dodd,
Mead & Co., New York, 1970.

WICKERSHAM, JAMES. *Old Yukon: Tales, Trails and Trials.*
Washington Lawbook Co., Seattle, 1938.

MORGAN, MURRAY. *One Man's Gold Rush—A Klondike
Album.* Photographs by E. A. Hegg. University of Washington Press, Seattle, 1967.

CAMPBELL, ROBERT. *Two Journals of Robert Campbell,
1830–1851.* Shorey Publications, Seattle, facsimile repro-
duction, 1958. (Campbell established the Hudson's Bay
Post of Fort Selkirk.)

BERG, AMOS. "Today on the Yukon Trail of 1898," in *National Geographic*, Vol. LVIII, No. 1 (July 1930). (Account of a canoe trip.)

15: Epilog: Twilight

Thus departed Hiawatha,
Hiawatha the Beloved,
In the glory of the sunset,
In the purple mists of evening,
To the regions of the home-wind,
Of the Northwest-Wind, Keewaydin,
To the Islands of the Blessed,
To the Kingdom of Ponemah,
To the Land of the Hereafter!

A flaming sun has dipped below the western shore. The mists begin to rise off a darkening lake to the accompaniment of swelling nightsounds. Somewhere, a loon cries. You and your crew savor the twilight, squatted around the flickering embers of the campfire. It will be a moment for remembering, and to be remembered. For the family that has made the extra-special commitment to the canoe tripper's environment, the rewards are not just here and now, but long lasting. These are the memories and the bonds forged more strongly on a foundation of shared experiences.

Canoeing and canoe tripping is a lifetime sport. Those of us who were introduced to the magical world as kids

A six- to eight-mile-an-hour current permitted us to cover many miles in a day, even with young kids. This is the Pelly River, well above its confluence with the Yukon River.

now have the means to rekindle within ourselves those earliest fantasies and the appreciation of simple pleasures. Living through one's kids may be an abhorrence on the Little League diamond, but in canoe tripping it is *de rigueur*. It's good form for fathers, mothers, grandfathers and uncles, too! But we've said all these things before. Pardon us if we press the theme too relentlessly. We hope we have conveyed some of the fun, and demonstrated the manifest rewards to be gained from the healthful activity of canoe tripping, but we would like to leave behind some final thoughts, as the last embers die in our little campfire.

As with the achievement of most things of lasting value, a commitment to a family canoe trip must be made at the outset. The commitment must be to building a foundation of knowledge and skills, and extending your family's canoeing endeavors as the foundation takes on the mantle

Canoe tripping with kids

of experience. To attack the project too zealously, to get caught up in born-again frontiersmanship, may create expectations doomed to frustration, or worse. A commitment to learning canoe skills and canoe safety, a commitment to modest excursions before tackling the ambitious, and a commitment to passing on the wilderness ethic to future generations, will be the key to a life-long love affair with the sport. It is a commitment like the sowing of a garden. There will be planning, selecting, cultivating—ever conscious of the weather—and contributing the sweat of one's brow. Perhaps you will have the good fortune of gentle rains and ample sunshine. If all is done well, there will be a bountiful harvest; in fact, many bountiful harvests.

In the purple mists of evening, and in many twilights to come (we make no representations with respect to the "land of the hereafter"), you and your tribe can savor experiences and memories, and be thankful to Hiawatha and his kin who made it all possible, floating on the water . . . "like a yellow leaf in Autumn . . ."

Information sources

Below is a partial listing of waterway guidebooks, and several map sources. The list just scratches the surface, however. In addition to available guidebooks and government map sources, there are periodicals, such as *Canoe* and *Backpacker–Wilderness Camping, The Canadian Geographic Journal, Outside,* and many others which can provide specific information or merely inspiration. Every state, including Alaska and Hawaii, boasts at least one canoe club (Pennsylvania, for example, has forty-five clubs or affiliations of interest to the canoeist or kayaker); and every state has a Department of Tourism, Park and Recreation Department and Department of Natural Resources ready to dispense information, which may be helpful to the canoeist.

For anyone planning a canoe, kayak or raft trip anywhere in North America, there is one definitive work entitled *Wilderness Waterways—A Guide to Information Sources,* by Ronald M. Ziegler, published by the Gale Research Co., 1979. Containing over 300 pages, the contents include "Reference Works," "Building and Repair," "History, Biography and Trip Accounts," "Waterways Guidebooks" (from which we have borrowed heavily for our list), "Basic List of Recommended Books," "National Canoeing, Kayaking, and Rafting Organizations," "Clubs and Affiliated Groups" (over 400 are listed by state), and "Map Sources." *Wilderness Waterways* would be a good investment for the trip planner, since it concentrates in one volume every conceivable source of information, organized by chapters and indexed.

We can't emphasize enough the importance—and fun— of planning and researching your trip. On the other hand, don't be put off by a lack of readily available information about a particular area. The harder you have to dig, the more likely you are to find a locale and a trip uniquely suited to your taste, and one which may not be overcrowded with other vacationers.

WATERWAYS GUIDEBOOKS

Appalachian Mountain Club. *The A.M.C. New England Canoeing Guide.* 3rd ed. Boston: 1971. 619 p.

———. *A.M.C. River Guide.* Vol. 1, *Northeastern New England.* Boston: 1976. 186 p. Preface.

AQUARDO, CHIP. *Canoeing the Brandywine: A Naturalist's Guide.* Chadds Ford, Pa.: Tri-County Conservancy of the Brandywine, 1973. 61 p. Paperbound.

BATCHELOR, BRUCE T. *Yukon Channel Charts: Sternwheeler-Style Strip Maps of the Historic Yukon River.* Whitehorse, Yukon Territory, Canada: Star Printing Co., 1975. 55 p. Paperbound.

BENNER, BOB. *Carolina Whitewater: A Canoeist's Guide to Western North Carolina.* 2d ed. Morganton, N.C.: Western Piedmont Community College, 1976. Distributed by Morganton, N.C.: Pisgah Providers. x, 164 p. Spiralbound.

A Boater's Guide to the Upper Yukon River. Rev. ed. Anchorage: Alaska Northwest Publishing Co., 1976. ix, 78 p. Paperbound.

BURMEISTER, WALTER F. *The Connecticut River and Its Tributaries.* Appalachian Waters, no. 6. Oakton, Va.: Appalachian Books, forthcoming.

———. *The Delaware River and Its Tributaries.* Appalachian Waters, no. 1. Oakton, Va.: Appalachian Books, 1974. vii, 274 p. Paperbound.

————. *The Hudson River and Its Tributaries.* Appalachian Waters, no. 2. Oakton, Va.: Appalachian Books, 1974. viii, 488 p. Paperbound.

————. *The Susquehanna River and Its Tributaries.* Appalachian Waters, no. 3. Oakton, Va.: Appalachian Books, 1975. viii, 600 p. Paperbound.

————. *The Southeastern U.S. Rivers.* Appalachian Waters, no. 4. Oakton, Va.: Appalachian Books, 1976. viii, 850 p. Paperbound.

BURRELL, BOB, and DAVIDSON, PAUL. *Wildwater West Virginia: A Paddler's Guide to the Whitewater Rivers of the Mountain State.* 2d ed. Parsons, W. Va.: McClain Printing Co., 1975. 160 p. Preface. Paperbound.

Canoe Sport British Columbia. *British Columbia Canoe Routes: A Guide to Ninety-Two Canoe Trips in Beautiful British Columbia.* Rev. ed. New Westminster, British Columbia: Nunaga Publishing Co., 1974. 111 p. Paperbound.

Canoe Trails of North-Central Wisconsin. Madison: Wisconsin Tales and Trails, 1973. 64 p. Paperbound.

Canoe Trails of Northeastern Wisconsin. Madison: Wisconsin Tales and Trails, 1972. 72 p. Paperbound.

Canoeing the Wild Rivers of Northwestern Wisconsin. 1969. Reprint. Eau Claire: Wisconsin Indian Head Country, 1977. Paperbound.

CARTER, RANDY. *Canoeing Whitewater River Guide.* 8th ed. Oakton, Va.: Appalachian Books, 1974. viii, 267 p. Preface. Paperbound.

CAWLEY, JAMES S., and CAWLEY, MARGARET. *Exploring the Little Rivers of New Jersey.* 3d ed. New Brunswick, N.J.: Rutgers University Press, 1971. xi, 251 p. Preface.

CLARK, FOGLE C. *Buffalo National River Guide.* University, Miss.: Recreational Publications, 1976. Map.

————. *Ozark Scenic Riverways Guide.* University, Miss.: Recreational Publications, 1977. Map.

COLWELL, ROBERT. *Introduction to Water Trails in America.* Harrisburg, Pa.: Stackpole Books, 1973. 221 p. Paperbound.

Connecticut River Watershed Council. *The Connecticut River Guide.* Rev. ed. Easthampton, Mass.: 1971. 87 p. Paperbound.

CORBETT, H. ROGER, JR. *Blue Ridge Voyages: One and Two Day River Cruises; Maryland, Virginia, West Virginia.* Blue Ridge Voyages, vol. 2. 2d ed. Oakton, Va.: Appalachian Books, 1972. iv, 84 p. Preface. Paperbound.

————. *One Day Cruises in Virginia and West Virginia.* Blue Ridge Voyages, vol. 3. Dunn Loring, Va.: Louis J. Matacia, 1972. vi, 116 p. Preface. Paperbound.

CORBETT, H. ROGER, JR., and MATACIA, LOUIS J., JR. *Blue Ridge Voyages: One and Two Day River Cruises; Maryland, Virginia, West Virginia.* Blue Ridge Voyages, vol. 1. 3d ed. Oakton, Va.: Appalachian Books, 1972. v, 75 p. Paperbound.

COUNCIL, CLYDE C. *Suwannee Country: A Canoeing, Boating, and Recreational Guide to Florida's Immortal Suwannee River.* Sarasota, Fla.: Council Co., 1976. 60 p. Paperbound.

DeHART, DON, and DeHART, VANGIE. *A Guide of the Yukon River.* Cheyenne, Wyo.: Cheyenne Litho, 1971. 47 p. Paperbound.

DENIS, KEITH. *Canoe Trails Through Quetico.* Quetico Foundation Series, no. 3. Toronto: Quetico Foundation, 1959. Distributed by Toronto: University of Toronto Press. ix, 84 p. Paperbound.

DUNCANSON, MICHAEL E. *A Canoeing Guide to the Indian Head Rivers of West Central Wisconsin.* Virginia, Minn.: W. A. Fisher Co., 1976. 61 p. Paperbound.

————. *Canoe Trails of Southern Wisconsin.* Madison: Wisconsin Tales and Trails, 1974. i, 64 p. Paperbound.

————. *A Paddler's Guide to the Boundary Waters Canoe Area.* Virginia, Minn.: W. A. Fisher Co., 1976. 76 p. Paperbound.

DWYER, ANN. *Canoeing Waters of California.* Kentfield, Calif.: GBH Press, 1973. 95 p. Preface. Paperbound.

ESSLEN, RAINER. *Back to Nature in Canoes: A Guide to American Waters.* Frenchtown, N.J.: Columbia Publishing Co., 1976. 345 p. Paperbound.

EVANS, LAURA, and BELKNAP, BUZZ. *Desolation River Guide.* Boulder City, Nev.: Westwater Books, 1974. 56 p. Paperbound.

————. *Dinosaur River Guide.* Boulder City, Nev.: Westwater Books, 1973. 64 p. Paperbound.

Farmington River Watershed Association. *The Farmington River and Watershed Guide.* Avon, Conn.: 1970. iii, 60 p. Preface. Paperbound.

Fédération Québécoise de Canot-Kayak. *Guide des Rivières du Québec.* Montreal: Messageries du Jour, 1973. 228 p. Preface. Paperbound.

FOSHEE, JOHN H. *Alabama Canoe Rides and Float Trips.* Huntsville, Ala.: Strode Publishers, 1975. 263 p. Paperbound.

FURRER, WERNER. *Kayak and Canoe Trips in Washington.* Lynnwood, Wash.: Signpost Publications, 1971. 32 p. Preface. Paperbound.

————. *Water Trails of Washington.* Lynnwood, Wash.: Signpost Publications, 1973. 31 p. Preface. Paperbound.

GABLER, RAY. *New England White Water River Guide.* New Canaan, Conn.: Tobey Publishing Co., 1975. iv, 236 p. Preface. Paperbound.

GARREN, JOHN. *Oregon River Tours.* Portland, Oreg.: Binford and Mort, 1974. ix, 120 p. Paperbound.

GRINNELL, LAWRENCE I. *Canoeable Waters of New York State and Vicinity.* New York: Pageant Press, 1956. viii, 349 p.

HAMBLIN, W. KENNETH, and RIGBY, J. KEITH. *Guidebook to the Colorado River, Part 1: Lees Ferry to Phantom Ranch in Grand Canyon National Park.* Brigham Young University Geology Studies, Studies for Students, no. 4.

2d ed. Provo, Utah: Brigham Young University, Department of Geology, 1969. 84 p. Preface. Paperbound.

————. *Guidebook to the Colorado River, Part 2: Phantom Ranch in Grand Canyon National Park to Lake Mead, Arizona–Nevada.* Brigham Young University Geology Studies, Studies for Students, no. 5. Provo, Utah: Brigham Young University, Department of Geology, 1969. ii, 126 p. Preface. Paperbound.

HARRIS, THOMAS. *Down the Wild Rivers: A Guide to the Streams of California.* 2d ed. San Francisco: Chronicle Books, 1973. 223 p. Paperbound.

HAWKSLEY, OSCAR. *Missouri Ozark Waterways.* Rev. ed. Jefferson City: Missouri Conservation Commission, 1976. 114 p. Preface. Paperbound.

HAYES, PHILIP T., and SIMMONS, GEORGE C. *River Runners' Guide to Dinosaur National Monument and Vicinity, with Emphasis on Geologic Features.* Rev. ed. Denver: Powell Society, 1973. 78 p. Paperbound.

HEDGES, HAROLD, and HEDGES, MARGARET. *Buffalo River Canoeing Guide.* Rev. ed. Little Rock, Ark.: Ozark Society, 1973. 14 p. Paperbound.

————. *The Mighty Mulberry: A Canoeing Guide.* Little Rock, Ark.: Ozark Society, 1974. 16 p. Paperbound.

HUSER, VERNE, and BELKNAP, BUZZ. *Snake River Guide.* Boulder City, Nev.: Westwater Books, 1972. 72 p. Paperbound.

Illinois Department of Conservation. *Illinois Canoeing Guide.* Springfield, Ill.: 1975. 67 p. Paperbound.

Indiana Department of Natural Resources. *Indiana Canoe Guide.* Indianapolis: 1975. 108 p. Paperbound.

JAMIESON, PAUL. *Adirondack Canoe Waters: North Flow.* Glens Falls, N.Y.: Adirondack Mountain Club, 1975. 299 p. Paperbound.

JENKINSON, MICHAEL. *Wild Rivers of North America.* New York: E. P. Dutton and Co., 1973. 413 p.

JONES, CHARLES, and KNAB, KLAUS. *American Wilderness, a Gousha Weekend Guide: Where to Go in the Nation's Wilderness, on Wild and Scenic Rivers and Along the Scenic Trails*. San Jose, Calif.: Gousha Publications, 1973. iv, 212 p. Paperbound.

KNUDSON, GEORGE E. "Guide to the Upper Iowa River." Decorah, Iowa: Luther College, 1970. vi, 57 p. Mimeographed.

MAKENS, JAMES C. *Makens' Guide to U.S. Canoe Trails*. Irving, Tex.: Le Voyageur Publishing Co., 1971. 110 p. Paperbound.

MARKS, HENRY, and RIGGS, GENE B. *Rivers of Florida*. Atlanta: Southern Press, 1974. 116 p. Paperbound.

MARTIN, CHARLES. *Sierra Whitewater: A Paddler's Guide to the Rivers of California's Sierra Nevada*. Sunnyvale, Calif.: Fiddleneck Press, 1974. 192 p. Paperbound.

MATACIA, LOUIS J., and CECIL, OWEN S. *Blue Ridge Voyages: An Illustrated Canoe Log of the Shenandoah River and Its South Fork*. Blue Ridge Voyages, no. 4. Oakton, Va.: Louis J. Matacia, 1974. 184 p. Paperbound.

MEYER, JOAN, and MEYER, BILL. *Canoe Trails of the Jersey Shore*. New Jersey Recreation Series. Ocean, N.J.: Specialty Press, 1974. v, 73 p. Preface. Paperbound.

Minnesota Department of Natural Resources. *Minnesota Voyageur Trails*. 1970. Reprint. St. Paul, Minn.: 1972. 48 p. Paperbound.

MITTENTHAL, SUZANNE MEYER. *The Baltimore Trail Book*. Baltimore, Md.: Greater Baltimore Group, Sierra Club, 1970. Distributed by Oakton, Va.: Appalachian Books. xi, 163 p. Paperbound.

MONTAGNE, JOHN DE LA. *Wilderness Boating on Yellowstone Lakes*. Bozeman: Montana State College, 1961. 31 p. Paperbound.

Mutschler, Felix E. *Desolation and Gray Canyons*. River Runners' Guide to the Canyons of the Green and Colorado Rivers, with Emphasis on Geologic Features, vol. 4. Powell Centennial, vol. 4. Denver: Powell Society, 1969. 85 p. Paperbound.

——. *Labyrinth, Stillwater, and Cataract Canyons*. River Runners' Guide to the Canyons of the Green and Colorado Rivers, with Emphasis on Geologic Features, vol. 2. Powell Centennial, vol. 2. Denver: Powell Society, 1969. 79 p. Paperbound.

——. *River Runners' Guide to Canyonlands National Park and Vicinity, with Emphasis on Geologic Features*. 2d ed. Denver: Powell Society, 1977. 99 p. Paperbound.

Nickels, Nick. "Canada Canoe Routes." Lakefield, Ontario: Canoecanada, 1973. 198 p. Preface. Mimeographed.

——. *Canoe Canada*. Toronto: Van Nostrand Reinhold, 1976. vi, 278 p. Preface. Paperbound.

Nolen, Ben M., ed. *Texas Rivers and Rapids*. Humble, Tex.: Nolen, 1974. 128 p. Paperbound.

North Central Canoe Trails. *Wisconsin's North Central Canoe Trails*. Rev. ed. Ladysmith, Wis.: 1967. ii, 28 p. Paperbound.

Nova Scotia Camping Association. "Canoe Routes of Nova Scotia," Halifax, Nova Scotia: 1967. 112 p. Mimeographed.

Ontario Voyageurs Kayak Club. "Ontario Voyageurs River Guide." Toronto: 1970. 150 p. Mimeographed.

Palmer, Timothy T. *Susquehanna Waterway: The West Branch in Lycoming County*. Williamsport, Pa.: Lycoming County Planning Commission, 1975. x, 56 p. Paperbound.

Palzer, Bob, and Palzer, Jody. *Whitewater, Quietwater: A Guide to the Wild Rivers of Wisconsin, Upper Michigan, and N.E. Minnesota*. 2d ed. Two Rivers, Wis.: Evergreen Paddleways, 1975. 157 p. Paperbound.

Parks Canada. *Wild Rivers: Saskatchewan.* Wild Rivers Series, no. 1. Ottawa: Department of Indian Affairs and Northern Development, Parks Canada, 1974. 66 p. Paperbound.

PATTERSON, BARBARA MCMARTIN. *Walks and Waterways: An Introduction to Adventure in the East Canada Creek and the West Branch of the Sacandaga River Sections of the Southern Adirondacks.* Glens Falls, N.Y.: Adirondack Mountain Club, 1974. 171 p. Paperbound.

PEWE, TROY LEWIS. *Colorado River Guidebook: A Geologic and Geographic Guide from Lees Ferry to Phantom Ranch, Arizona.* Tempe: Arizona State University Press, 1969. 78 p. Paperbound.

PIGGOTT, MARGARET H. *Discover Southeast Alaska with Pack and Paddle.* Seattle, Wash: The Mountaineers, 1974. 269 p. Paperbound.

RIGBY, J. KEITH, et al. *Guidebook to the Colorado River, Part 3: Moab to Hite, Utah, through Canyonlands National Park.* Brigham Young University Geology Studies, Studies for Students, no. 6. Provo, Utah: Brigham Young University, Department of Geology, 1971. 91 p. Preface. Paperbound.

ROBINSON, WILLIAM M., JR. *Maryland–Pennsylvania Countryside Canoe Trails: Central Maryland Trips.* Oakton, Va.: Appalachian Books, 1974. iii, 34 p. Paperbound.

SATTERFIELD, ARCHIE. *The Yukon River Trail Guide.* Harrisburg, Pa.: Stackpole Books, 1975. 159 p. Paperbound.

SCHWEIKER, ROIOLI. *Canoe Camping Vermont and New Hampshire Rivers: A Guide to 600 Miles of Rivers for a Day, Weekend, or Week of Canoeing.* Edited by Catherine J. Baker. Somersworth: New Hampshire Publishing Co., 1977. vi, 91 p. Paperbound.

SCHWIND, RICHARD. *West Coast River Touring: Rogue River Canyon and South.* Beaverton, Oreg.: Touchstone Press, 1974. 221 p. Preface. Paperbound.

SCOTT, IAN and KERR, MAVIS. *Canoeing in Ontario.* Toronto: Greey de Pencier Publications, 1975. 80 p. Paperbound.

SEA EXPLORERS. Ship 648, comps. *Canoeing in Louisiana.* Edited by John W. Thieret. Lafayette, La.: Lafayette Natural History Museum, 1972. iv, 62 p. Preface. Paperbound.

SIMMONS, GEORGE C., and GASKILL, DAVID L. *Marble Gorge and Grand Canyon.* River Runners' Guide to the Canyons of the Green and Colorado Rivers, with Emphasis on Geologic Features, Powell Centennial, vol. 3. Denver: Powell Society, 1969. 132 p. Paperbound.

SPINDT, KATHERINE M., and SHAW, MARY, eds. *Canoeing Guide: Western Pennsylvania and Northern West Virginia.* 6th ed. Pittsburgh, Pa.: American Youth Hostels, Pittsburgh Council, 1975. viii, 168 p. Paperbound.

Texas Explorers Club. "Suggested River Trips Through the Rio Grande River Canyons in the Big Bend Region of Texas." Rev. ed. Temple, Tex.: 1971. 30 p. Mimeographed.

Texas Parks and Wildlife Department. Trail and Waterways Section. *An Analysis of Texas Waterways: A Report on the Physical Characteristics of Rivers, Streams, and Bayous in Texas.* Austin, Tex.: 1972. 240 p. Paperbound.

THOMAS, EBEN. *Hot Blood and Wet Paddles: A Guide to Canoe Racing in Maine and New Hampshire.* Hallowell, Maine: Hallowell Printing Co., 1974. viii, 188 p. Paperbound.

———. *No Horns Blowing: A Guide to Canoeing 10 Great Rivers in Maine.* Hallowell, Maine: Hallowell Printing Co., 1973. ix, 134 p. Paperbound.

———. *The Weekender: A Guide to Family Canoeing.* Hallowell, Maine: Hallowell Printing Co., 1975. vi, 134 p. Paperbound.

Thomson, John Seabury. *Potomac White Water: A Guide to Safe Canoeing above Washington, Seneca to Little Falls.* Oakton, Va.; Appalachian Books, 1974. 44 p. Paperbound.

Truesdell, William G. *A Guide to the Wilderness Waterway of the Everglades National Park.* Coral Gables, Fla.: University of Miami Press, published in cooperation with the Everglades Natural History Association. 1969. 64 p. Paperbound.

Ungnade, Herbert E. *Guide to the New Mexico Mountains.* 2d ed. Albuquerque: University of New Mexico Press, 1972. 235 p.

Vierling, Philip E. *Illinois Country Canoe Trails: Des Plaines River.* Chicago: Illinois Country Outdoor Guides, 1976. 72 p. Paperbound.

————. *Illinois Country Canoe Trails: Du Page River, Kankakee River, Aux Sable Creek, Des Plaines River.* Chicago: Illinois Country Outdoor Guides, 1975. 84 p. Paperbound.

————. *Illinois Country Canoe Trails: Fox River, Mazon River, Vermilion River, Little Vermilion River.* Chicago: Illinois Country Outdoor Guides, 1974. 80 p. Paperbound.

Weber, Sepp. *Wild Rivers of Alaska.* Anchorage: Alaska Northwest Publishing Co., 1976. vi, 170 p. Paperbound.

Youghiogheny River Guide. Columbus, Ohio: Rich Designs, 1975. Map.

Wheat Ridge High School, Jefferson County, Colorado. "River Rats' Guide to the Green and Yampa Rivers: Dinosaur National Monument, Colorado-Utah." Denver: Colorado Outward Bound School, 1972. 24 p. Mimeographed.

Index

AMATEUR THEATRICALS, 152
Animal tracks. *See under*
Wildlife, tracks and
tracking

BEES, 163–164
Berton, Pierre, 19, 181–184
(*ill.*, 183)
Blackflies, 160–162, 164
Boots and shoes. *See under*
Clothing for canoeing,
footwear

CAMPS AND CAMPING
base camp, 139–140, 146
campsites, 140–145
chores, 146–147
Canoeing
children's abilities, 122
cross draw, 115–117 (*ills.*,
113, 116)
draw stroke, 110 (*ill.*, 111),
114
entering, exiting, canoe, 106
(*ill.*)
"J" stroke, 107, 109–110
(*ill.*, 109)
learning the strokes,
120–124
lining, 119–120 (*ill.*, 120)
power stroke, 107

quartering, 113–114 (*ill.*,
114)
rapids, 112, 113
setting around a bend,
117–118 (*ill.*, 116)
stern pry, 107, 108 (*ill.*),
114–115 (*ills.*, 115, 116)
stern sweep, 110 (*ill.*, 111)
upstream ferry, 118–119
(*ill.*, 118)
Canoes
best number for trips,
100–101
designs, 39
freeboard, 102 (*ill.*, 101)
loading, 101
materials, 40–41
"paddleability," 39
paddles, 41–44 (*ills.*, 42, 43)
size and weight, 40, 41
stability, 39, 101
trim in the water, 101–102
(*ill.*, 101)
See also Packs and packing
Chiggers, 162–163, 164
Children
adaptability of, 13
best age to start canoe
tripping, 9, 13
trip activities for, 147–156
Clothing for canoeing
children's clothing
checklist, 64–65

children's special needs, 58, 60
choice influenced by activity, 60
colors, 60
footwear, 61
hats, 61, 63
layered dressing, 59
materials, 59
rain gear, 62–63 (*ill., 62*)
suppliers, 65
Conditioning for canoe tripping, 97–98
Cooking equipment. *See under* Food for canoe trips

Diary-keeping, 174

Emergencies and hazards
high water, 96, 117
hypothermia, 93–94
reversals, 97
souse holes, 97
strainers and sweepers, 96, 117
weirs, 97
Equipment for canoeing
bottom pads, 102
canoe car racks, 37–38 (*ills., 38*)
equipment checklist, 56–57
importance of durability, 37
life jackets, 44–45 (*ills., 45*)
sleeping bags, 52–53
sleeping mats, 51–52
tents, 49–51 (*ills., 50*)
tools, 53–55
See also Canoes

Family feeling, aided by canoeing, 8
First aid
bibliography, 97
checklist, 98–99
kit, 91–92 (*ill., 92*), 95
physical exam, 90
Red Cross course, 90, 96
See also Emergencies and hazards
Fishing, 147–149 (*ills., 147, 148, 149*)
Flies, 162, 164
Food for canoe trips
bannock, 74–75 (*ill., 74*)
basic food groups, 67–68
camp food suppliers, 82
clean-up, 78–79
cooking equipment, 71–72, 75
fires and fire-building, 77–78
food box (*wanigan*), 70 (*ill.*)
food supply checklist, 80–82
freeze-dried camp foods, 68, 69
gorp, 76
long trips, 69
packing food, 68–69, 70–71
planning food for children, 66
shortcake, 73
short trips, 66–67
"smores," 77
stuffed fish, 76

Gold-panning, 154–155 (*ill., 154*)

Home movies, 174–175

Hypothermia. *See under*
  Emergencies and hazards

INSECT PESTS. *See under*
  INSECTS, BY NAME

LAKES
  route-finding on, 130–133
  wind a problem on, 112–113,
    131

MAPS, 18–19, 25, 127, 130–133
  (*ill., 132*)
Mosquitoes, 158–159, 164

NO-SEE-UMS, 159–160, 164

OUTFITTERS, 19, 26–27
Ozark Mountains (Missouri),
  20–28

PACKS AND PACKING
  "Dry Box," 49
  for no-portage trips, 45
  for portage trips, 45
  packing strategy, 47, 105
  types, 46 (*ills., 46, 47*)
Paddles. *See under* Canoes
Planning a canoe trip
  calculating costs, 27–28
  duration of trip, 16
  information sources, 17–20,
    21–28, 189–199
  location of trip, 17–18, 104
  mileage, 104

timing of trip, 16–17
trial run for beginners, 15
  See also Maps; Portages and
    portaging; Travel with
    children
Photography, 175–179
Portages and portaging
  canoe-carrying, 135–138
    (*ills., 137*)
  mosquitoes, 159
  packs, best for, 134
  planning for, 104, 105
  portage yoke, 136 (*ill.*)

RAFT-BUILDING, 153 (*ill.*)
Rain, 165–168
Rain gear. *See under* Clothing
  for canoeing
Rivers
  current-reading, 117,
    128–129
  large, 117–119
  small, 114–115
Route finding, 127–128,
  130–133
Role models, for children, 8

SCORPIONS, 164
Snakes, 165
Spiders, 163, 164
Swimming, 152

TICKS, 162–163
Travel with children
  entertaining children, 31–35
  packing car, 30, 32
  very long trips, 33–34

WANIGAN. *See under* FOOD
   FOR CANOE TRIPS, FOOD
   BOX
Wasps, 163–164
Waterways guides, 18–19, 21,
   190–199
Whittling, 152 (*ill.*)
Wildlife
  bears, 86
  beavers, 87

introducing children to,
   84–85
moose, 87–88
otters, 87
raccoons, 86–87
tracks and tracking, 149–151
Wind, 112–113, 168–170

YUKON RIVER, 180–184

Index